MW01008629

CRAVING
MY
RIVAL

BY P. RAYNE

CRAVING MY RIVAL

THE MAFIA ACADEMY

P. RAYNE

AVON

An Imprint of HarperCollins Publishers

This is a work of fiction. Names, characters, places, and incidents are products of the author's imagination or are used fictitiously and are not to be construed as real. Any resemblance to actual events, locales, organizations, or persons, living or dead, is entirely coincidental.

CRAVING MY RIVAL. Copyright © 2023 by Piper Rayne. Bonus epilogue copyright © 2023 by Piper Rayne. All rights reserved. Printed in the United States of America. No part of this book may be used or reproduced in any manner whatsoever without written permission except in the case of brief quotations embodied in critical articles and reviews. For information, address HarperCollins Publishers, 195 Broadway, New York, NY 10007.

HarperCollins books may be purchased for educational, business, or sales promotional use. For information, please email the Special Markets Department at SPsales@harpercollins.com.

Avon, Avon & logo, and Avon Books & logo are registered trademarks of HarperCollins Publishers in the United States of America and other countries.

Originally published as *Craving My Rival* in the United States in 2023 by Piper Rayne Incorporated. Epilogue originally published online in 2023.

FIRST AVON PAPERBACK EDITION PUBLISHED APRIL 2025.

Interior text design by Diahann Sturge-Campbell

Interior art © Oleksandr/Stock.Adobe.com

Library of Congress Cataloging-in-Publication Data has been applied for.

ISBN 978-0-06-341252-1

25 26 27 28 29 LBC 5 4 3 2 1

HB 01.29.2025 0647

To all the "good girls"

AUTHOR'S NOTE

This book contains references to content that may be upsetting to some readers. Trigger warnings include alcohol, attempted murder, murder, profanity, sexually explicit scenes, stalking, physical violence, and gun violence. Reader discretion is advised.

PLAYLIST

Here's a list of songs that inspired us while we were writing *Craving My Rival*.

Miss World – Hole
ocean eyes – Billie Eilish
Paint the Town Red – Doja Cat
Rich Flex – Drake & 21 Savage
Don't Look Back in Anger – Oasis (Remastered)
Slow Poison – The Bravery
Love Lies – Khalid & Normani
Sex, Drugs, Etc. – Beach Weather
bad idea right? – Olivia Rodrigo
Boom – Anjulie
The Great War – Taylor Swift
this is what falling in love feels like – JVKE

SICURO ACADEMY — ITALIAN CRIME FAMILIES

Northeast Territory

Specializes in running weapons
Marcelo Costa
(head of the Costa crime family)

Southeast Territory

Specializes in counterfeit rings and embezzlement schemes
Antonio La Rosa
(next in line to run the La Rosa crime family)

Southwest Territory

Specializes in drug trafficking and money laundering
Dante Accardi
(next in line to run the Accardi crime family)

Northwest Territory

Specializes in securities fraud and cyber warfare
Gabriele Vitale
(head of the Vitale crime family)

CHAPTER ONE
DANTE

My dad calls me into his office a couple of days into Thanksgiving break. I enter the wood-paneled room in our family's Calabasas estate and pause. He's alone and sitting on his couch. Generally, we're joined here by his consigliere—the underboss—or at the very least some capos to discuss business, and he's always behind his desk.

My dad works constantly, as most dons do. There's a lot to do when you're the boss of your crime family, but he never sits back to enjoy the fruits of his labor. Thankfully, I do that enough for the both of us.

I learned at the age of four to always close his office door behind me.

I turn to face him, and something about his demeanor puts me on edge. His scowl is the same as the time I crashed my Ferrari, but it doesn't appear to be directed at me this time.

"What's up?" I sit in the plush chair across from him.

"There's news we need to discuss." He gestures to the box of cigars open on the table between us.

I shake my head. I hate cigars and hope they die out when my generation takes over. "Figured that's why I was summoned."

The sternness of his face reads, "cut the sarcasm." Aldo Accardi is all business, all of the time. People probably wonder if I'm really his rightful heir, we're so different. I do what needs to be done, but after, I enjoy myself.

"You're aware of all our problems with the Russians lately. Not just our family but the other three families as well."

I nod.

Of course I know. Shit got crazy at the private college I attend with all the other Mafia academy kids about a month ago, and it ended in the death of one of the Vitales and a few of the Russians. Sicuro Academy was founded by four Italian Mafia families—the La Rosas, the Costas, the Vitales, and us, the Accardis—as a place of safety for the new generation. Now, thanks to what happened on campus, our lives have become carnage off campus—a war between the Italians and Russians.

"Many men have died on both sides. Good soldiers. A war between Mafia factions is not good for business."

"I know." I lean forward, placing my forearms on my knees.

"We must put an end to it before it becomes a full-scale war and draws more attention from the authorities than it already has. Drastic measures must be taken."

"Agreed."

Fuck the Russians. None of this would have started if they hadn't kidnapped Aria Costa. We should take them all out and be done with it. Let them see who they're fucking with. It's probably the only thing us and the other three Italian crime families agree on.

I'm still in the dark as to why the Russians took Aria Costa. I helped Gabriele Vitale rescue her because I owed him a favor, but we don't ask the whys. I'm just happy my debt has been paid.

"I'm glad you understand the nature of the situation and agree that we need to take unusual measures."

"Tell me what you need and consider it done." I wonder who he's having me take out. I hope it's before I return to campus.

"That's what I like to hear. Family first at all times . . ."

I take a deep breath. That doesn't sound like orders to take out someone. More like I grabbed the short stick even though I wasn't playing.

"I've arranged your marriage."

My mouth dries, and I blink over and over. In our world, arranged marriages are common, and I knew one day this conversation would happen. But there's no one I'm aware of from any of the families, including ours, who would add benefit to my dad's position or our family.

"Jesus, calm down. Look at you." He stands, goes over to the bar, pours a whiskey, places it in front of me, and sits back down.

I gulp down half and wipe my mouth. "Who?"

A look of pity crosses his face. "Polina Aminoff."

I swipe the glass off the table and pound down the rest of the drink.

"Her brother Dmitri Aminoff and I arranged it."

"A Bratva princess?"

He draws a cigar out of the box. "Yes."

I bolt up off the seat. "I refuse!"

He shows no reaction, taking the cutter to the end of the cigar and bringing the cigar to his mouth as if it's a leisurely Sunday after our big family dinner.

"You do?" he asks around the cigar.

"You've lost your fucking mind!"

He stops with the match at the tip of his cigar, his brown eyes searing into mine. "Remember who you're speaking to, figlio."

I grind my teeth, hands fisted, while he lights his cigar, puffing out the first inhale to get it lit. "Why would you make me marry a Russian?"

"Sit," he says.

I do, running my palms down my thighs to calm myself.

"It's the only way to ensure a path to peace." He rests his ankle on his opposite knee, leaning back on the couch.

"Not after I strangle the fucking bitch. Polina is a queen bee. And again, she's fucking Russian."

My dad sucks on his cigar, blowing out a puff of smoke. "I understand this isn't ideal, but this is duty. For *all* the families. Your marriage secures an alliance with the strongest Russian Bratva family, signaling to all the other Bratva families that an attack against the Accardis is an attack against the Aminoffs. Things have escalated too far between all the Russian and Italian families. This marriage will de-escalate them. Once Polina bears your children, even more so."

I can't stomach the thought. Polina is hot as fuck, but I've never thought of her as anything more than the enemy.

"Why can't someone else do it?" I hear the whine in my voice, but I don't care one fucking bit.

"You're the last one destined to be a don available. Marcelo Costa is engaged to Mirabella La Rosa, Antonio La Rosa is married to that Sofia girl, and Gabriele Vitale and Aria Costa were wed yesterday in a small ceremony, I'm told."

I lean back in the chair and cross my arms. "No big grand Italian wedding? She's probably knocked up."

"Perhaps. Regardless, this is your duty to fulfill. It will make some of our present issues go away, and it will make the Italians indebted to us, only working to our advantage. Down the road, as the bloodlines mix, it may even result in us being able to work with the Russians instead of against them."

I bite my cheek. Un-fucking-believable. I'm the last one standing, so I get stuck with the Russian bitch for life.

"Stop looking like it's a death sentence, Dante. You'll get married and produce some heirs. All the while, you can continue your recreational activities. Just make sure it's done in private." He arches an eyebrow.

He looks at me as though I should bend down and kiss his pinkie ring, thankful that he's giving me permission not to be faithful when it's pretty much a way of life for the men in our world. Very few remain faithful to their wives.

That's not what I'm concerned about, though. I'm going to be tied to a woman who I have no doubt will make my life miserable. He can't expect me to open up a bottle of our best champagne to celebrate.

I stand from the chair. "This is bullshit."

I start for the door, but my father calls my name with the same authority he directs at his made men. I spin to face him.

"You will do this. And you will do it with a smile. The agreement is tenuous at best. Do not fuck it up for the families."

I say nothing and storm out of his office. I stomp down the grandiose hallway, having no idea where I'm going, but I need to escape. I need to release some of this fucking stress.

* * *

I END UP at Misfits, one of the strip clubs outside of Calabasas and closer to downtown Los Angeles, with a stripper named Candy bobbing on the end of my dick. My father owns the club, and I'm sure he'll hear about my appearance, but I don't care.

"That's it, you slut, take it. Deeper." My hand winds through her bleached hair, and I push her down on my cock until she's gagging.

When I pull her off, saliva runs down her chin, and her eyes glint with satisfaction. This isn't Candy's and my first encounter. A little name-calling and degradation always gets her off.

I push her head back onto my length and let her do what she does best. It certainly isn't dancing on stage, but she's got one hell of a gag reflex, or lack thereof.

She bobs up and down, and I try to sink down to that euphoric place where everything fades away, where all that consumes me is pleasure, but I'm struggling. Every time I close my eyes, all I see is a pair of sky-blue irises.

Eyes that belong to Polina Aminoff, my soon-to-be fiancée.

I shake my head, opening my eyes. Fuck that. She will not ruin this for me. She's already set to ruin my life. I don't know Polina—at all—but her reputation precedes her. She's a Bratva brat, through and through.

And so while Marcelo, Antonio, and Gabriele all get to continue their bloodlines with a woman from our world, I'm forced to procreate with our biggest rival. Fuck me.

I tighten my grip in Candy's hair, and the hearty moan she lets out isn't one of dissatisfaction. Rather than closing my eyes and seeing that set of eyes again, I focus on Candy's handiwork.

That does the trick because, within a couple of minutes, my nuts are ready to bust.

"Get ready to swallow, whore," I warn her because I'm nothing if not a gentleman.

I come down the back of her throat, and she takes it all, like always. My hand releases her hair, and her mouth pops off my dick, licking the rest of the mess off her lips.

Two people settle on either side of me.

"You know Dad hates it when you fuck around with the girls." My younger brother, Dom, says as he sits on my left.

"Yeah, but Candy here loves it, don't you?" I smack her round juicy ass as she stands. "Get back to work."

She turns with her bottom lip jutted out in a pout but does as she's told.

"Candy, save some for me later," my cousin Santino, on my right, says.

She looks at him over her shoulder and gives him a big smile.

"What are you guys doing here?" I ask, putting my dick away and zipping up my pants.

"Dad told us to find you. Said you stormed out and didn't want you to do anything stupid," my brother says.

I suppress my eye roll. "He wants you to make sure I don't have a temper tantrum?"

"Basically," Santino says.

The DJ announces a new girl to the stage, and my attention shifts her way.

"Did he tell you why I was mad?" I ask without taking my eyes off the brunette strutting onstage.

"Nope. Just told us you were pissed. This is the first place we looked," Santino says.

"Am I that predictable?" I grumble.

"Pretty much," Dom says with a shrug.

I sigh, not that either of them can hear it over the music. "I have to marry Polina Aminoff."

Neither of them says anything for almost a full minute.

Santino is the first one to speak. "Sorry, I thought you said that you have to marry a Russian."

He says the word Russian with such distaste it suggests he understands why I'm here.

"You heard correctly." I fist my hand in my lap.

Dom lets out a low whistle. "Why the hell do you have to do that?"

I recap my conversation with my father, and again, they're silent.

"This has disaster written all over it," Dom says.

He's right, because he knows me. I tend to act like a child when I don't get my way. So it might end in mine or Polina's death. And I'm not talking some *Romeo and Juliet* shit.

CHAPTER TWO
POLINA

My older brother Dmitri flawlessly took over as the head of the Bratva last month after my oldest brother, Feliks, was murdered. Dmitri has held a confident air with the men as if he was made for this role. But right now, Dmitri sits across from me in the living room of our New York City brownstone, looking as if he's coming down with the flu.

He's just finished explaining to me the state of things in our world and how the Russians are on the verge of war with the Italians—as we should be. They killed our fucking brother.

"Why do I need to know all of this?" I'm a woman. We aren't involved in the family business, never have been. This better not be his way of telling me he's putting around-the-clock security on me while we're on Thanksgiving break. Or forbidding me to leave the brownstone. I'll go mad in this house.

Dmitri shares a look with my twin brother, Pavel, sitting to my right, and that unnerves me. Does Pavel know something I don't? Did he contrive something with Dmitri?

"I was talking to the four Italian family heads, and a decision has been made." Dmitri looks at the fireplace on the right. The family photo there is from years earlier when we were all just children, and my dad was the second-highest man in the Bratva.

I scowl. "You're working with the Italians now? After they murdered Feliks?"

He should scold me for my outburst and tone. Feliks would have.

But Dmitri doesn't, which makes me think he doesn't want to upset me. Which has me assuming this is very bad news he's about to deliver.

He sighs and looks at me with sympathetic eyes. "It's what's best for all involved."

I roll my eyes and gesture with my hand for him to get on with it.

"Sestronka, it has been arranged that you will marry Dante Accardi, next in line to run the Accardi crime family."

I blink rapidly, the words settling like a boulder in quicksand. "Funny joke. Come on, just tell me."

"This is no joke," Dmitri says.

I look at Pavel, whose eyes gleam with satisfaction, and nausea churns in my stomach. If he's happy about it, then it's true, because nothing makes him happier than watching me suffer.

I spring off the couch. "I am not marrying Dante Accardi!" My hands fist at my sides, my fingernails digging into my palms.

"I understand that this is surprising. But joining the two families, the two nationalities, will help to forge a tenuous peace. Then we can all get back to business."

"You want me to marry an Italian? Who is also Sicuro's biggest manwhore?" I thread my fingers into my long blond hair.

I've never spoken to Dante, but everyone on campus knows him. He's probably fucked half of campus already. He's definitely worked his way through the Roma House.

"These are difficult times. The power within us has transitioned twice now in recent years, and our foothold at the top of this organization is anything but secure. If we're the ones to help forge peace between all the factions, we'll be seen as invaluable and won't have to worry so much about a threat to our leadership."

He might as well be speaking Mandarin to me because what he's saying doesn't make sense to me. Because none of it matters. The fact is he's telling me I have to marry our enemy.

"I'm not marrying Dante Accardi." My voice is firm. Final.

Dmitri looks at me with pitying eyes.

"You've never been asked to do a fucking thing in your life to help this family," Pavel says.

I shift my gaze to my twin brother. His sky-blue eyes that match my own are narrowed as if he wants me to challenge him.

Everyone always thought that Feliks was the one to be afraid of—the oldest brother, the enforcer—but my experience was different. Pavel is a wolf in sheep's clothing, though I'm the only one who knows what he's capable of.

I ignore Pavel and shift my focus to Dmitri. He's the head of this family now and the sibling I've always been closest to.

"Dima, please don't make me do this." I hate the fact I'm begging and sound desperate. It reminds me too much of—nope. Not going there.

"It's already done. We'll be meeting the Accardis at the private airstrip when we return to the Sicuro Academy in two days. Dante will offer you a ring, and you will accept it." He pins me with a stare. Maybe he can be hard on me, too, because he resembles Feliks right now.

It's clear to me that there is no changing his mind. While Feliks always acted on emotion, Dmitri is the stalwart, logical one. He doesn't do anything without thinking it through.

I suck back my rare show of emotion, pissed I even let it be seen in the first place, and regain my usual cool aloofness. "When are we to be married?"

"This coming summer. After the end of this school year."

I'll only have my freedom for nine months at the most, six months if I'm really unlucky.

I've never thought too much about marriage. I'm not one of those girls who has dreamed of her wedding since she was young. Let's face it—in our world, I knew I could be arranged with someone. But one thing I'd always assumed was that I'd be marrying a Russian.

The Italians have a hard-on for arranged marriages, but in the Bratva, it's not as common. Not unheard of, but not mainstream.

Now I'm going to be forced to marry a man I'm sure hates me as much as I hate him, bear his children, and be around his family, who surely will not welcome me with open arms. I'll be leaving one nightmare for another.

I clear my throat. "Can I leave now?"

Dmitri gives me a small frown and nods. I don't even bother looking, knowing that Pavel is likely gloating, basking in my misery.

I make my way to the door slowly, careful not to run out of the room the way I want to. I maintain my pace all the way to the third level, where my bedroom is. Once I'm behind locked doors, I allow the tears to fall.

It's not a new lesson that I can't trust any man. But it hurts, nonetheless. Dmitri and I have always been close, and for him to force me to do this . . . it's like a betrayal.

I have no idea why I'm not used to them by now.

CHAPTER THREE
DANTE

Our private plane touches down at the airport near the Sicuro Academy.

"Ready to meet your lady love?" Dom asks, laughing.

"Fuck off."

I'm no closer to accepting my fate than the day my dad told me, and my mood is sour. The ring I'm to give Polina today burns against my thigh in the pocket of my pants.

"C'mon, at least she's hot," Dom adds, not knowing when to keep his fucking mouth shut before I shut it for him.

"Must be nice to have no expectations put upon you," I sneer.

Sure, Dom has to do some of the same dirty work as me, but there's not a magnifying glass on his life. There's a good chance that no one will ever tell him who to marry since he's second in line.

Santino eyes Dom from the seat across from us. "You need to learn when to tread lightly."

Dom only laughs.

I'm quiet as the plane slows, eventually coming to a stop. The door opens, and I unbuckle, standing to make my way out. Everything around me is in slow motion because everything in my life is about to change and not for the better.

I'm not *afraid* to marry her. I don't fear much honestly, and I can get Polina in line a lot easier than any of the other founding four guys. They picked the right guy for the job, even if I was the only one left standing.

So I do what I do best. I straighten my back, hold my head high, and walk down the steps of my family's private plane. I appear to be the man now in charge of Polina's destiny on my way to where Dmitri, Pavel, and Polina stand.

Dom was right about one thing—she's stunning. Wavy blond hair that reaches the top of her breasts, creamy skin, and blue eyes as bright as the cloudless winter sky overhead. She's wearing a puffy designer jacket and black pants that look as if they're painted on, black boots with cream-colored socks sticking out above them. She'll probably cost me a fortune to dress, but at least she'll look gorgeous on my arm.

I purposely take my time making my way over to the group while my brother and Santino follow me. The Russian brothers eye me somewhat warily, while Polina's face is as cold and indifferent as a doll that can't blink. When I reach them, I nod in greeting. I'm sure as fuck not going to say it's good to see them because it's not.

Dmitri breaks the silence, as he should. From rumors, he's doing well taking over the job after his brother's murder. "I think we can all agree that this is uncomfortable for everyone, but we appreciate you meeting us, don't we, Polina?"

She looks at him from the corner of her eye, not saying a word, then sets her eyes on me. Dmitri sighs.

Dom shifts to my right, and Pavel's hand goes to his hip. That's fine. We're armed, too. Though our weapons will be confiscated the moment we hit campus security, there was no chance we were arriving at this meeting without being armed.

"Let's just get on with this," I say.

"I've arranged for you and Polina to have your own ride back to campus. That way you can get to know one another better." Dmitri motions to a blacked-out SUV parked off to the left.

Normally I'd demand to use ours, but using their car is a better option than making Santino and Dom ride with Pavel to campus. The fact that Dmitri's going to put his little sister inside of this vehicle tells me it's not rigged with explosives. Unless he's a completely heartless son of a bitch—which could be a possibility, but the pity in his eyes when he looks at his sister tells me no.

"And so we can arrive on campus together and appear as a united front." I voice what he's not saying.

Dmitri nods. "There's that, too."

I hold out my arm, directing Polina to go ahead of me. "Shall we?"

She doesn't move, so I walk over, open the car door, and motion for Polina to get inside. She's still standing with her brothers. I hold her stare until she walks over and climbs inside the SUV. My insistence that she go first is not just chivalry. It's so that in case there is an explosive rigged to this thing, I'm not the only one inside.

I get in the back and shut the door. She's shoved herself all the way over to the other side, enough so that her right hip is probably touching the door.

Her entire demeanor spurs me to assume that when it comes time to fuck her, she'll probably lie there stone-faced and silent, not moving, like the frigid bitch she is. Awesome. Can't wait for a lifetime of that.

The car pulls away, and neither of us says anything for a few minutes. It almost feels as though it's a game, and whoever speaks first loses. But I have something to do, and my father will have something to say if I don't do it. So I reach into my pocket and pull out the ring box. It weighs heavily in my hand.

I open the black velvet box and pull out the five-carat cushion-cut diamond. I told my mom to pick something out, given that I didn't even know this woman or what she'd like, nor would I care anyway.

"Here, this is for you to wear." I hold it out across the space between us.

Her gaze flicks down to the ring, and her jaw tightens, the hands resting on her thighs forming into fists. She doesn't make any movement to take the ring.

"Just take it. We're both stuck in this shit situation, and you being a stubborn bitch about wearing this ring isn't going to change anything."

"Such sweet words," she hisses. "Is this how you work your magic with so many ladies?"

"You asking around about me, tesoro?"

Her pale skin glows on her face, and I find I love getting a rise out of her. It will be a nice outlet for my frustration.

"Hardly. Your manwhore status is pretty well cemented at the academy."

I'm surprised to find that her Russian accent is more sexy than annoying. It's not particularly thick—she's likely spent too much time in the US for that to be the case—but it's noticeable.

"Aw, it's okay to be jealous you haven't been on the receiving end of my cock yet. Don't worry, we have a lifetime for you to worship it."

She finally looks at me. I can see why she's earned the reputation as queen bitch of the Moskva House. Her regard is withering and might make a lesser man shrink.

"You'll be the one on your knees, I assure you."

Her comment stuns me, and I bark out a laugh. "We'll see about that."

I can set aside my anger about the situation long enough to admit that she's beautiful. I'm not blind. And she might think she can lead me around by the dick, but she doesn't know who she's dealing with. I'll never let my life and my decisions be ruled by pussy, especially Russian pussy.

"Yes, we will." Her voice is still void of emotion. She turns and looks out the window.

I realize she still hasn't taken the ring from me, so I grab her wrist, yanking it toward me. Her head whips back in my direction, and there's fear in her eyes, but it's gone so quickly I could've imagined it. This woman doesn't appear to fear much.

"Put this on your finger, and don't take it off." I shove it down her left ring finger.

As soon as it's nestled in place, she yanks her hand back to her lap.

"You should be thanking me and telling me what a beautiful piece of jewelry it is."

"Why would I thank you for putting handcuffs on me?" She glares at the ring in distaste.

I give her the same grin that pissed her off earlier. "Tesoro, if I put handcuffs on you one day, you'll probably enjoy it, believe me."

She rolls her eyes and shoots me the same annoyed look she has had since the plane landed. I only laugh.

We don't speak during the rest of the drive to the Sicuro Academy. After we've gone through security and relinquished our cell phones and my gun, the SUV rolls into the roundabout to drop us off.

The vehicle stops, and I expect she'll jump out to flee me. Instead, she turns to look at me. "We may be stuck in this situation, but I say you do what and who you want, and I'll do the same."

I shrug. "Works for me."

"We may be forced to marry each other, but that doesn't mean we have to talk, or even see each other, prior to the wedding."

"Agreed." I nod.

"Then it's decided. See you at the altar." She whips back and opens the door, stepping out without a backward glance in my direction.

And though I should feel happy she's given me the okay to continue my usual life, at least for the rest of the school year, I'm annoyed that I'm so easy for her to cast aside.

CHAPTER FOUR
POLINA

I walk out of the SUV and head straight to Moskva House without a backward glance at my new fiancé. I despise him, not only because he likely had a role in killing my brother and was an enemy even before that, but because he represents my future. A future I don't want.

But even though I hate him, my body isn't cooperating. Sitting so close to him, inhaling his masculine scent, I found myself oddly attracted to him.

It would be hard to argue he isn't attractive. What with his light blue eyes and light brown hair that falls perfectly just above his ears in a sort of wavy curl that most women would kill to have. His thick lashes and the warm glow of his skin remind me of the sun.

Still, the betrayal of my body annoys me. When he spoke to me the way he did—a way no guy ever has before, for fear of my brothers—the space between my thighs tingled.

Whatever. Get yourself together, Polina. Do not let him see you rattled.

I walk into Moskva House wearing a mask of indifference, even though I feel like the sacrificial lamb to the other three Bratva families as everyone watches me enter.

Do they know about my engagement? Why can't one of their daughters marry Dante Accardi to keep the peace?

I continue ignoring them as I make my way to the elevator. I reach out with my left hand and stab the up button, the overhead lights glinting on my new piece of jewelry.

It really is a beautiful ring, but it's not like I'd admit that.

"So it is true?" Irina's voice comes from behind me.

I whip around to find her and Oksana gawking at me. They're the two friends I'm closest to here, but I don't trust either of them. I keep them in check with my mean girl tactics and have no doubt that at the first opportunity they'd attempt to take me down.

"What's true?" I arch an eyebrow. If she's not going to have the balls to ask me outright, I won't make it easy for her.

"You're engaged?" Oksana asks.

"To Dante Accardi?" Irina motions to the ring on my finger.

"I am." I raise my chin a touch, daring them to say anything about it. They're not idiots, they know I'm not happy about it, but I will not confide in these two.

"I didn't see that one coming," Oksana says with a slight smirk.

"Well, you wouldn't, given that your father is only in the working unit." I give her a saccharine smile, and her smug eyes fall to her feet. "It's for the good of all the families. Someone had to step up and do something before the bloodshed continues. It's not ideal, but I'll do what I must to keep us all safe."

That's a load of horse shit, but they don't need to know that. If I have to cast myself in the role of martyr, I will.

"That's good of you to think of everyone else," Irina says. She's just being sweet so I don't put her in her place the way I did Oksana.

"Now if you'll excuse me, I've had a long day of travel, and I'm going to go to my room."

The elevator dings. I don't wait for either of them to respond, stepping inside and pressing the button for my floor. Then I move to the back of the elevator, sigh, and let my head rest.

Putting up this unaffected air in front of everyone every time Dante is brought up will be exhausting, but I should be used to it by now.

* * *

Two weeks have passed since I returned to the academy after Thanksgiving break. Thankfully, Dante has stayed true to his word, and we've had no interaction.

He's stayed with his kind and I with mine.

Sure, I pass by him sometimes in the dining hall, but we don't acknowledge each other. It's enough that I've been branded with this stupid ring, serving as a reminder of my fate every day.

There's a party tonight in the abandoned caretaker building, and I plan on letting off steam and having fun. Unfortunately, other factions will be there, too—I overheard some of the Irish and the Italians talking about it in the dining hall today. Was everyone lectured on break to play nice? At least I doubt the cartel will be there. They usually stick to themselves.

I apply the pink gloss to my full lips in the mirror and double-check nothing is out of place. Part of the carefully crafted face I present to the world. Once I'm satisfied I look the part, I go to my closet and grab my jacket and gloves. It's a twenty-five-minute walk across campus to the abandoned lodge, and while it hasn't snowed yet, it's cold out.

A knock on my door sounds, and I expect it to be Oksana or Irina since they're meeting me here to head over to the party. But I swing the door open to find my brother Pavel.

My stomach instantly bottoms out. "What are you doing here?" I don't bother hiding the disgust in my voice.

"Where's Irina?"

I roll my eyes, though I'm filled with relief he's not here for me.

He and Irina have been on-again, off-again for years. I don't know what she sees in him. Most likely just a step up the Bratva ladder. A smarter girl would go for Dmitri.

"She'll be here any second. She, Oksana, and I are going to that party across campus."

"Why does she need to go to a party? She's got me."

I refrain from throwing up on his shoes. I guess they're on again.

"You'll have to ask her, but I'd be happy to make a list of whys if you'd like." I shouldn't taunt him, but the words slip out of my mouth.

Pavel grabs my wrist, his fingers digging into my flesh, but thankfully Irina shows up. "Lapushka, what are you doing here?"

He drops my wrist and beams at Irina and Oksana. "Looking for you. What's this I hear about you going to a party?"

Irina's gaze flicks to me. I don't react. She's the idiot who tried keeping it from him. She knows how controlling he is.

"I was going to text you. I just wanted to check with Polina first to know what time we're going." Irina runs her hand up his chest.

Her excuse is lame, but Pavel seems satisfied with her answer.

"You both ready to go?" I zip up my coat and put on my gloves.

"Yep," Oksana says.

Pavel takes the hand that's trailing up his chest by the wrist, tugging it down. "I don't feel like going to a party tonight."

Irina's gaze bounces to me, and I roll my eyes, already knowing she's ditching us.

"Have fun doing nothing." I step past them out of my dorm room and wait for everyone to exit before I lock my door.

Pavel doesn't say goodbye but rather drags Irina off in the opposite direction than we're heading.

I'm sorry, she mouths over her shoulder.

"She needs to figure out that the sun doesn't rise and set with your brother," Oksana says as we step into the elevator. "I'm surprised she went with him. She was excited to go tonight."

I shrug. "Her loss. What's in the bag?" I nod toward the large tote slung over her shoulder.

With a grin, she reaches in and pulls out a bottle of Belvedere vodka.

"Nice," I say. I was hoping I wouldn't have to drink shitty warm keg beer or bad whiskey to get a buzz going tonight.

We make the trek through the dark over the rolling landscape of the campus, using the flashlights on our school-issued phones to guide us when necessary.

When we hear the bass thumping from the music playing, we know we're close. I'm never sure how they sneak in the sound system for these things, but I don't care enough to ask anyone who might know the answer.

This isn't my first time at a party here. While the Italians have their forest parties, Russians have these. But then the Irish found out about our parties, and soon we didn't have the exclusivity we wanted.

The old caretaker's house is a two-story building that's seen better days. The school no longer maintains the residence, so it's become slightly derelict. Some of the old furniture remains, although I'd never sit on a piece. And the electricity still works, but only a few rooms have bulbs that haven't burned out yet. The worst part is no running water.

We step inside, and it's clear from the wall-to-wall people that we're some of the last ones to arrive. The Russians are separate from the Irish, as well as from the Italians, but even within the three groups, there's the separation of the different families.

Don't get me wrong, the Russians stick with the Russians if it comes down to it, but the four Bratva families aren't exactly tight. It's a very "the enemy of my enemy is my friend" vibe.

We make our way through the crowd in what was probably once the living room while some Drake and 21 Savage song thumps so loudly I can feel the bass through my body.

When we reach the rest of the people associated with the Aminoff family, Oksana pulls the vodka out of her bag. The two of us sipped straight from the bottle on the way here, so I'm already feeling warmth spread from my stomach outward to all my limbs.

Anyone who can't take straight vodka is either weak or not Russian.

"Want me to mix us a couple of drinks?" she asks me loudly enough so I can hear her over the music. She's pointing toward bottles of soda and juice in the kitchen. Nothing but the best for the country's elite.

"Sure, but make mine a strong one."

She nods and sets off toward the kitchen, bottle of vodka in hand.

I'm only standing there for a minute before Sasha Andreyev approaches me. He's a year older, and his father is pretty high up in our Bratva, working in the security group. Sasha's been after me since I was fourteen. I've made it clear to him that I'm not interested, but he can't seem to help but test his fortune with me every few months. I'm sure he's heard the rumors.

"Privet, kotik."

"I've told you before that I'm not your kitten, Sasha."

He grins, ignoring my glare.

Sasha is a good-looking guy—his hair is dark blond, and he has deep blue eyes—and I'm sure a lot of girls here think the same. But I learned a long time ago that the prettier the package, the uglier the inside.

"I heard the news," he says.

"News?" I arch my eyebrow, turning away from him to face the crowd again.

He picks up my left hand so the sparkling diamond is in view.

"Yes, I'm a happily engaged woman now. Time for you to move on, I suppose."

His jaw tics. "Are you really going to go through with marrying that khuy?"

"That's what the ring suggests." I don't want to have this conversation with him. I'm surprised it's the first time he's mentioned it, but then again, he's been off campus for whatever reason for over a week.

"Here you go." Oksana returns and hands me my drink.

I take it and swallow a large gulp.

"Seems your fiancé's commitment is flagging compared to yours." Sasha points to his left, and I follow his line of sight.

Dante is dancing to the song blasting through the room, grinding up against a girl I recognize as Italian. The plastic of my drink cup indents as my hand squeezes too hard.

"He can do what he wants for the time being, as can I." I keep my voice controlled, void of emotion, but I shouldn't have allowed my jealousy to show at all.

Dante is tall, but the girl he's dancing with is petite and curvy. I don't know why that bugs me. Maybe because I'm long and lithe, and the idea that he prefers her body type to mine makes me feel less than. As though he'll never be satisfied with me and will constantly seek out someone like her once we're married. Even though I should not care.

"Interesting," Sasha says.

"There's nothing interesting about it. Find something else to gossip about." I sip my drink.

He raises his hands in defense before one of his friends steals his attention.

Oksana and I watch everyone dancing in the middle of the living room. She keeps opening her mouth then shutting it—probably wanting to see if I'm upset watching my fiancé grind his dick against some other girl's ass. We might be friends, but I don't confide in her or anyone.

At one point, Dante catches my eye, and I see a gleam of something in his, almost as if he's enjoying me being forced to watch his performance with the little slut.

What makes me angrier than anything is that it bothers me. But that has to be because he's trying to embarrass me and make me look stupid and weak in front of everyone. I don't feel any kind of claim on Dante Accardi.

Maybe it's time to turn the tables. He's going to make me look like a fool? Two can play that game.

CHAPTER FIVE
DANTE

Isabelle grinds her ass against me as the beat of the music thrums through the house.

We've hooked up before, but we've never been anything serious. She knows how it is and accepts it, which is what makes her a good booty call.

For the fucking life of me, I don't know why I can't get any excitement going when I look down at her small body, her ass, and all those curves. I used to love that shit, favor it, but now . . . I don't know. Lately my jack-off sessions have focused on long, lean dancer-like bodies and modest curves.

I look across the dimly lit room at my fiancée draped over some Russian asshole as they dance. Fucking hell, I've been picturing her body naked and didn't even realize it.

I spotted Polina watching Isabelle and I dancing a half hour ago, though it was hard to tell whether she even cared. She had on that same bitchy perma-scowl she always does. For a split second, guilt shot through me, but why? We have an agreement, and I'm just living up to it.

She's free to do what she wants, as am I.

Only, watching her drape herself all over this guy and seeing him grinning at her as though she hung the fucking moon sours my mood. I might not care about her, but she's mine. She's been publicly declared as mine, and everyone knows it. It doesn't sit well with me that everyone in this house is watching her get all worked up with some other guy.

The guy's hands wrap around her waist to rest at her back. I watch as they slip lower, and lower, and lower, until they grab her ass.

I'm about to tell Isabelle to take a hike and storm over there when Polina whispers something into his ear and steps away from him. He nods, then she turns in my direction, walking toward us.

Perfect, let's see how she likes the up-close version of my partner's and my moves.

Pretending not to watch Polina, I rest my hands on Isabelle's hips, and she backs up even more, pressing her lush ass against my junk. I'm sure she's wondering why I'm not as aroused as I usually am.

Polina is almost to us . . . then she bolts forward, spilling her drink all down the front of Isabelle's white shirt.

"Oh, I'm sorry, suka. My bad." She bats her eyes and looks at Isabelle's shirt with a sly smile. It obviously wasn't an accident.

"Oh my god. Look what you did!" Isabelle instantly stops dancing and looks down at herself. "You did that on purpose."

Polina's expression doesn't budge. "I don't know what you're talking about. Someone jostled me as I made my way through the crowd." Her expression dares Isabelle to call her out.

Isabelle turns to face me instead. "I'm going to have to go back to Roma House to change. Come with me?" She looks at Polina and continues. "We can ditch the party and find something better to do."

Damn, I didn't know Isabelle had the nerve, but she's throwing down with Polina Aminoff. I can't help but be slightly impressed.

My gaze flicks to Polina. I want to see her reaction to Isabelle's blatant proposition. But her expression never changes. I shouldn't be surprised. I wonder what Polina looks like when she cracks a smile.

Jesus fuck. What do I have to do to rattle this woman?

"I'm gonna stay here," I tell Isabelle without taking my eyes off Polina.

"Seriously?" There's anger in Isabelle's tone, but I still don't remove my eyes from the Russian princess.

"Yeah, I have some things to deal with." Then I do look down at Isabelle. "Depending on how late it is, maybe I'll swing by your place when I make it back to the dorm."

She half smiles, not fully satisfied with my answer, but she'll continue hooking up with me for however long I want it to happen. "All right." She walks her fingers up my chest. "Just don't make it too late. I have to do some of my volunteer hours tomorrow morning."

"All right."

Isabelle pushes through the crowd, and I shift my attention back to Polina, but she's gone.

What the hell? Where did she go?

I'm tall enough to glance over the heads of most of the people here, but I don't see Polina. Then I notice someone with black leggings and black boots going up the stairs. Even though I see only the bottom half of their body, I'm sure it's Polina.

I push through the crowd until I reach the stairs, then I weave around people lingering on my way up until I'm standing on the landing. The hallway is full of people, but I spot a head of blond hair at the far end.

She turns and spots me, then disappears. It's not until I reach the end of the hallway that I realize there's a set of stairs leading up to what I assume is an attic. I take them two at a time until I reach the top and find her at the far end of the empty room, looking out the window.

The roofline is pitched, so I walk down the center of the room toward her. I'm too tall to walk without crouching anywhere else.

"Are you playing a game of cat and mouse? You should know that I always catch my prey," I say as I approach her.

"It's no game," she says without turning around. Her voice has thawed a bit compared to how she usually sounds.

"Seemed that way downstairs when you purposely spilled your drink all over Isabelle." I stand behind her and to her left and see the way her jaw tenses when I say Isabelle's name. Interesting.

"Accidents happen."

I trail the knuckle of my middle finger down her arm. "That's too bad. I was thinking maybe you were jealous and trying to get rid of the competition."

She laughs, but there's no humor in her voice. "Don't flatter yourself. Besides, there's no competition. You're *engaged* to me."

The way she says the word with just a small amount of possessiveness makes my dick twitch. I want to ask what the fuck that was, as if my dick can give me an explanation.

"A little competition is never a bad thing. How about I source a blow-up pool and some oil, and then you can really show Isabelle what's up?"

She looks at me over her shoulder. "You're a pig."

I lean in over her shoulder so our cheeks are almost touching. "You have no idea."

Her breath catches and holds for a heartbeat before she releases it. Then she schools her features again. "I'll have to remember your stance on competition the next time Sasha approaches me."

My eyebrows draw down. "That's the stronzo you were dancing with down there?"

"Yup. He's wanted me forever, and I haven't caved. Haven't really wanted to . . . until now."

I grind my teeth so as not to say something stupid. "We don't know each other, but I took you for a smart woman. Giving it to a lesser man than me wouldn't be a smart decision on your part."

The corners of her lips tip up slightly. "Sounds like something someone who's afraid of a little competition would say."

Before I can consider my actions, I grab her hip and wheel her around to face me. She gazes up at me in shock with big, wide eyes. Finally, some fucking emotion on her face. Leaning in and resting my hands on either side of the window behind her, I cage her in.

"You're a little Bratva brat who needs to be taught some manners. But don't worry, I know how to teach you. The next time you use that mouth against me for evil instead of good"—I punctuate the word good with a thrust of my hips into her stomach, showcasing my hard cock—"I'm going to bend you over my knee and spank you."

Her eyes flare wider, and her heavy lids drop down before she glares at me again. "I don't know how you Italians are used to talking to your women, but you need a few lessons in decorum." The breathy quality of her words gives her away.

A slow smirk transforms my face. "You telling me that cunt of yours isn't dripping wet and throbbing for me right now at the image of me spanking your bare ass?"

Her hand whips across my face, followed by a stinging sensation on my cheek.

I'd rather it be my hand spanking her ass and teaching her a lesson, but I take satisfaction in being the one to crack her shell and peer into the woman behind the hard, frigid layer she shows to the world.

I laugh and that incites her further. She pushes against my chest, but I don't budge. I grab her wrists and hold her to me.

"Truth hurts, tesoro."

She pulls at my grip. "Get your hands off me."

"C'mon now. You're my fiancée. It's quite a shame I haven't gotten a taste of you yet, don't you think?" I trail my nose down the side of her face, inhaling her scent. It has a powdery note with a woodsy undertone, far different from the floral crap I'm used to smelling on women.

"I'm not kissing you." She yanks at my grip to free her hands.

"Oh, you'll do more than that, I promise you. We have heirs to produce, remember?"

At the horrified expression on her face, I laugh and drop her hands. She rushes around me toward the stairs.

Part of me—a bigger part than I care to admit—wants to stop her from leaving, keep her here, and continue to get a rise out of her.

But I have to check myself. I'm getting far too much enjoyment out of our banter. Fiancée or not, she's still my enemy.

CHAPTER SIX
POLINA

A few days have passed since the party, and thankfully, I haven't run into Dante.

I want to rip out my hair when I remember how he affected me, how my perfectly curated mask shattered at his feet. Not only that, but he'd known. He somehow knew that his words affected me.

Never in my life have crude words been spoken to me. I should have been horrified by his filthy mouth, but my nipples pebbled, and my panties grew damp between my legs. What is wrong with me?

I should be repulsed and turned off, but when he whispered about how wet I was, all I wanted was for him to check for himself. For him to break that barrier, his large finger gliding along my soaked black thong, dipping under the silk, and sliding through my slick folds.

Blowing out a breath, I concentrate on what Irina is going on about across from me in the dining hall.

Oksana is seated beside her, and she says, "I think you should wear the green one, don't you think, Polina?"

They both turn to me, waiting for me to give my opinion.

"Yeah, definitely."

Irina frowns. "You've been somewhere else since the weekend. Everything okay?" She tilts her head in a way that makes her question come off as condescending, as if she's talking to a child. "I heard that Dante and that Isabelle girl were all over each other at the party. I wish I'd been there to support you."

The faux concern on her face makes me want to smack it off, like I smacked Dante on Saturday night. Irina might have managed to get her dig in, but she should know by now that I'll yank that knife out of my chest and rip her to shreds with it.

"I understand why you couldn't be there. God knows if you don't fuck my brother when, where, and how he demands, he'll get bored of you and move on just as he has every other time. Don't worry about it." I give her my best unaffected smile. *Bitch.*

The pitying smile that had been directed toward me slips.

"Right, well . . . if you ever need to talk, you know we're here, right?" Oksana says, trying to smooth the waters from the hurricane that's just landed on shore.

Both my brothers arrive at the table. Thankfully, Pavel sits beside Irina while Dmitri sits to my left.

"How's it going, sis?" Dmitri asks, studying me.

"Swimmingly, why wouldn't it be?" I give him a fake smile that even a blind man could see through.

He sighs and shakes his head. "It will get better."

"Save your fake platitudes. We both know that's not true."

"It is what it is, but if he steps out of line in any threatening way, be sure to let me know."

I reply with a curt nod. The idea of telling my brother the way Dante spoke to me this weekend crosses my mind. Maybe he'd get in trouble from his father. If I'm lucky, maybe his father would beat the shit out of him. But I don't bother because then I'd have to explain why Dante thought I was turned on and pray that I was a good enough liar to make it believable when I said that wasn't true.

"You guys coming to the Christmas Eve party?" Pavel asks Irina and Oksana.

"Haven't you already invited your pseudo-girlfriend here?" I ask him.

He levels a cruel and assessing gaze on me.

"We'll be there, won't we, Irina?" Oksana asks.

"Wouldn't miss it." She smiles, but it doesn't reach her eyes.

Every Christmas Eve, my family hosts a gathering in our brownstone. It's really more of a party than a Christmas celebration given that our Orthodox Christmas is in January, but it's usually a fun time.

Shouting from the far end of the dining hall draws our attention. I lean back in my seat and see that one of the members of the Volkov family is having words with someone from the La Rosa family.

The Sicuro Academy has a zero-tolerance policy, but a lot of good that's done over the past year. Everything is always covered up by the student body. People might go "missing," but they're not really. Someone here always knows where the bodies are buried. But no one is a rat, and they'd never squeal to the authorities.

Regardless of whether they know exactly what happened, the administration has been more diligent than ever in ensuring that any unrest is quickly squashed and that consequences are enacted quickly. I heard that one of the cartel members and an Irish guy were expelled last week just for hurling insults at each other. It didn't even get physical.

Some of the students slowly rise from their seats. When I can no longer see anymore, I stand on my chair to watch. The Italian swings first, hitting the other guy in the jaw, but he doesn't go down. They trade blows while the entire student body jeers and chants. When they both go to the floor, they're blocked from my sight, and I see some of the staff headed in their direction.

I'm about to step off the chair when the side of my face tingles with awareness.

I look to find Dante staring at me. I hold his gaze for a beat, but I spot Sasha walking toward me, so I turn my attention from my fiancé to Sasha, greeting him with a big smile.

"Can you help me down?"

His eyes widen at my request. He's surprised but pleased. Sasha takes my waist in both hands, lifting me and lowering me to the floor.

"Thanks."

"Anytime, kotik."

I don't scold him this time for using the nickname. I motion to the table. "Have you eaten yet? Want to join us?"

He sits beside me while the teachers break up the fight. I have no doubt that's the last I'll see of those two guys on campus.

For the rest of the meal, I'd swear Dante's gaze is on my back, but when I stand to leave and sneak a peek over my shoulder, he's gone. It shouldn't cause my stomach to sink, but it does.

CHAPTER SEVEN
DANTE

We've been away from school on holiday break for a few days. I haven't seen much of my dad because he's been out of the house a lot, so it's not a surprise that on the one morning he's here, I'm summoned to his office. I'm sure he just wants an update on how things have been with Polina.

What am I going to tell him? That we don't talk at all, and on the rare occasion we do, we bicker, and I'm pretty sure the banter makes both of us horny, though neither would ever admit it?

His office door is closed when I arrive, probably because he's been working since five this morning. I just got out of the shower and got dressed. It drives my dad crazy when I sleep late and laze around in the morning.

I knock, and he tells me to come in, so I swing the door open and come to a stop. For the second time in two months, I'm in disbelief when entering my father's office. He's not alone.

Polina sits on one couch by herself, and her brothers sit on the couch directly opposite her. Sitting in the armchairs at one end of the two couches is my father and his consigliere, Joey Gervais.

"Sit next to your fiancée, son." My father gestures to the empty spot beside Polina.

Slowly, I step forward, assessing the situation. The energy in the room is tense, and Polina's expression is her usual cold indifference. She doesn't bother to look at me as I take a seat beside her; rather she stares straight ahead between her brothers.

"What's this about?" I ask.

Dmitri gives my dad a nod, clearly deferring to my father since it's his house.

"I got word about the fight in the dining hall at Sicuro between an Italian and a Russian."

I raise both hands. "It was the La Rosas. I didn't have anything to do with that."

My father tips his chin down and looks at me from under his eyebrows, clearly displeased. "Let me finish."

I remain quiet.

"In addition to that, we've had more incidents of violence in the real world. Just a day ago, both of us lost soldiers." He nods in Dmitri's direction. "It would seem that our hope that this engagement might help to bring peace hasn't come to fruition."

Fucking perfect. I'm free.

"Well, I guess that's that then. We gave it a good try, right?" I stand and look down at Polina. "Keep the ring."

"Sit down, Dante." My dad's voice is lethal.

Begrudgingly, I sit back down beside my still-fiancée.

"This just means that it's time to step up our efforts. I've heard from Dmitri that the two of you don't spend any time together at all. Neither of you act like an engaged couple. There's no show of acceptance and understanding between our two sides, no show of peace."

I glare at Dmitri. Fucking rat. Why is he still at the academy? He should be out in the real world, running his family.

"Don't look at him like that," Polina snipes beside me.

I whip my head in her direction and narrow my eyes.

"Polina," Dmitri warns.

Pavel stifles a laugh, and Dmitri shifts his attention to his brother. Man, I might not be able to control my fiancée, but Dmitri can't control his entire family.

My dad stares at Polina before he intervenes. "If the two of you can't set an example for everyone to follow, then what hope do we have of setting the tone between our factions?"

I refuse to admit that he has a point, so I lean back, silent with my arms crossed, legs spread wide.

"I asked Dmitri to make the trip out here because things are changing from this point forward," Dad says.

I sit up straight, my elbows resting on my knees.

Dmitri says, "You two need to spend time together, be seen in public, and appear to be a happily engaged couple."

I scoff. When no one says anything, I realize they're serious.

"What do you think?" I ask Polina, angling my body her way because there's no way she's happy about this, yet she's here.

She deems me worthy of a response, I suppose, because she turns her head to look at me. "I'm as thrilled as you are probably."

"When you're back at school, you will be expected to spend time together the way a real engaged couple would," my dad dictates.

"And you'll attend our Orthodox Christmas celebration at our home in New York," Dmitri adds.

My mouth drops open. "I might as well put my own head on a stake. The hell I'm walking into a room full of Russians all by myself and without any weapons."

Dmitri hasn't expressed that I can't have weapons, but he doesn't have to. These three were checked thoroughly before they were allowed into the house today. I'm sure the Russians will be no different.

"Yes, you will, Dante. You will have Dmitri and Pavel's protection. No one will harm you while you're there." My dad leans back and sips his whiskey.

Easy for him to say when he'll be back here in California. Am I that disposable to him? God, this fucking blows.

Sure, I enjoy getting a rise out of Polina and pushing her until she cracks, but that doesn't mean I want to spend time with her.

"Whatever," I grind out between clenched teeth.

"You'll return to the academy for a few days after Christmas break. Since Orthodox Christmas falls on a weekend, you will fly out to New York on Friday evening and return on Sunday. I've already spoken with the chancellor to let him know."

I chuckle. "I'm sure he appreciated the call from you during his break."

"He's just as eager as any of us to put these tensions aside."

"Fine." Not fine, but I can't disobey my father—especially in front of others. "I'm not sleeping there, though."

No way am I going to sleep in their house. They'd probably sneak in and slit my throat in the middle of the night.

Dmitri sighs. "You will be safe."

I look at him and Pavel, who's been oddly quiet this whole time. "No offense, but your word means shit to me."

Pavel goes to rise off the couch, but Dmitri puts a hand on his chest and forces him to sit down. I don't miss the way Polina stiffens next to me.

"I'll be staying at a hotel." My voice is firm and final.

"I think that's acceptable." For once, my father throws me a fucking bone.

"I'm concerned that if anyone finds out he's not staying in the house, they'll be suspicious of the union," Dmitri is quick to argue.

"They won't," Polina says.

Dmitri gives her a look.

"Fair enough," my dad says. "What if Polina stays with Dante at the hotel?"

Polina whips her head in my father's direction. "I'm not going to allow people to think I'm another one of your son's whores who puts out for him on demand."

My father's jaw clenches, and his brows draw. He does not allow women to talk to him like that. Why hasn't someone put her in line before now? I get that her father died five years ago, but she should have known by then not to raise her voice to any male, especially a don. If this continues, and I do end up marrying her, my father will expect me to put her in line.

This time, my dad eyes Dmitri with an expression that says, *Handle this, or I will.*

"Sestronka, you two are engaged to be married. No one is going to think of you as a whore," Dmitri says gently.

"Dante can book a suite. You can have your own room inside it," Joey speaks for the first time. Maybe he's here as a show of support so that my father isn't outnumbered by the Russians.

Polina says nothing, just crosses her arms and leans farther back into the couch. I suppose that's as good as an agreement from her.

"It's settled then." My dad claps his hands in front of him and stands. "These two will turn things around when they're back on campus." He gives me a meaningful look. "Dmitri, you'll keep me updated."

So now I have Polina's big brother playing my babysitter. This is bullshit.

Regardless, I want this meeting to end, so I don't say anything, just nod like a good little boy while inside I'm fuming.

And when the three of them finally leave, I thank my lucky stars my dad didn't suggest that Polina stay and celebrate Christmas with us.

CHAPTER EIGHT
POLINA

Dante and I are flying back to New York tonight.

I'm dreading this weekend. The idea of parading Dante around on my arm in front of everyone stings. Still, I have to play along. After we left the Accardis, I begged Dmitri to call off the whole thing, not make me do this, but he was insistent we had no choice. I'm not sure why, but I get the sense that there's more than just mending relationships between the Italians and Russians on the line, even though Dmitri didn't say that.

Dante and I are silent on the drive to the airport. Neither one of us wants to be here, though I suspect him even more so, being that he's walking into the heart of enemy territory.

By the time the private plane takes off from the airport, we've still somehow managed not to share a word with each other. At this point, it feels like a silent standoff, and whoever talks first is the weaker one.

Once we're at flying altitude, I lean my head back in the seat and close my eyes, hoping to drift off for the duration of the flight to make the uncomfortable tension more tolerable.

"There's a bed in the back you can use. I'm happy to tuck you in," Dante says.

It's childish, but a part of me preens that he's the one to break the silence. It feels like a small victory.

I open my eyes and look at him in the seat kitty-corner to me. "I'll pass, thanks."

"You sure? I've been told I'm really good at it." He winks.

He's only saying it to irritate me, and I'm annoyed with myself that he succeeds because I can't brush off his words like I can everyone else's.

"Well, you've had a big enough sample size to know for sure."

He chuckles. "Careful, tesoro, that sounds a little like jealousy."

"Am I going to be subjected to this the entire flight to New York? Warn me now. Maybe I'll take a sedative."

"You trying to pretend you don't like my mouth now? After I saw you staring at it like you wanted to feel it on you at the party? When the words that came out of it made you wet?" He doesn't divert his gaze, waiting for a reaction from me.

How does he make it seem so easy to say all . . . that and not be fazed? It's not like I'm some innocent virgin or anything, but there are some things you don't say. Unless you're Dante Accardi.

But I refuse, outright refuse, to show him that his words make me uncomfortable while at the same time make me yearn for more of them to be directed at me.

"Is there a reason the only words that come out of your mouth when you're around me are sexual innuendos? Is that all you're capable of? Grunting out crude words? Should I expect there to be minimal conversation in our marriage? Maybe instead of a boy toy, I'll have to find someone to have an adult conversation with." I smile serenely at him.

His nostrils flare, and I inwardly score another point for me because I've touched a nerve. He's quiet for a beat, but I should have known nothing will shut him up.

He sips his drink and leans back comfortably in his seat. "Fine. Tell me what to expect tomorrow."

"You've never done Christmas before?" I arch an eyebrow, keeping my expression neutral.

"I've never done a *Russian* Orthodox Christmas before."

I shrug. "It's probably not all that different from whatever you do. All my family and friends will be there. We'll eat a big feast, exchange some presents, maybe sing Christmas carols, stuff like that."

He nods and shrugs. He's so transparent when his thoughts are turning over in his head.

"What?"

"I just thought it would be a lot different than what we do."

I roll my eyes. He's an idiot. "Because we're *so* different?"

He shrugs again. "Maybe."

"We all want the same thing, Dante. We're not that different." I unbuckle my seat belt and go to the back to lie down until it's time to land.

I don't want to sit with him and have a "getting to know you" session.

* * *

WE ARRIVE IN New York, and one of my brother's soldiers picks us up, driving us to the hotel where we'll be sharing a suite.

I can't believe I have to stay in the same suite as Dante, even if there are two bedrooms. I understand why he wouldn't want to stay in my family home, though. You're at your most vulnerable when you're sleeping, and to do so in the middle of enemy territory would just be stupid.

The Bratva member hands our bags off to the bellhop while we go inside.

Being with Dante on my own is strange. I know we only flew a few hours to get here, but being out in public, in the real world outside of the Sicuro Academy, feels weird. Like this is really real, and this is what I can expect for the rest of my life, the two of us moving about in the world.

We approach the reception desk, and the woman looks up, her gaze drifting to Dante first. A slow, appreciative smile creeps onto her face. She spares me no more than a cursory glance.

I suppose this is something I'll have to get used to—women appreciating Dante's looks.

"Hello, sir. How can I help you?" Her voice is practically a purr, and I seethe.

It's not that I'm jealous. I'm not. It's that I'm standing right here, and she's being completely obvious about flirting with my fiancé. Under the normal circumstances of being engaged, it would mean I loved this man. The blatant disrespect she's showing me is like a nagging itch under my skin, but I school my features, not willing to say anything because I don't want Dante to read anything more into my reaction.

"We're here to check in," Dante says, using one of his charming smiles.

The woman appears so captivated by his beauty that she can't form thoughts because she just stares across the counter at him.

"If you're done eye-fucking my fiancé, we'd really like the key to our suite now." The words are out of my mouth before I can stop myself.

Dante turns to me, but I refuse to look in his direction.

The receptionist's cheeks pinken. "Of course. My apologies. Name?"

Dante tries to suppress his grin and gives some bullshit name. You don't want your enemies to be able to call up the hotel and confirm that you're staying there.

She types away, and within a minute or so, she holds out two key cards toward us. I snatch the cards from her hands and don't bother responding when she bids us farewell.

Walking toward the elevators, I don't wait for Dante to follow, but of course within a few steps, he's right beside me. I can practically hear the humorous words he wants to unleash as we wait silently for the elevator.

"What?" I snipe.

"Nothing." The amusement is laced in his voice.

"Whatever," I mumble. I'm tired and bitchy, and I just want to go to bed, get tomorrow over with, and get back to the academy.

"I like a woman who fights for what's hers."

I roll my eyes as the elevator dings. "Good to know."

We don't say anything as the elevator lifts to our floor, but the small space quickly fills with his scent. His mix of expensive cologne and a smell I suspect is wholly him accosts me from every angle, and an ache builds between my legs.

The elevator dings for our floor, and I rush out of the confined box.

Dante follows me down the hall to our room, and I feel his gaze on me the entire time, wandering from my legs to my ass and up to my ponytail swinging back and forth. When I reach the door, Dante cages me in, his front to my back. He towers over me, and I close my eyes to find my equilibrium as he scans the card over the lock. The light turns green, and he twists the handle, opening the door for me.

It's a beautiful suite decorated in dark walnut furniture with light upholstery and draperies. There's a large living room with an adjoining dining room and an open-concept kitchenette.

I walk farther in to investigate the bathroom and to pick my bedroom, but I stop and look back. There must be another hallway somewhere. I turn and head in the other direction, but there are no other doors. So I go back to where I was and stare at the one bed in the one bedroom.

"What the hell?" I almost scream.

"Looks like we'll share a bed sooner than we thought."

Dante's voice startles me, and I whip around.

"Not a chance. Call the front desk, and fix this." I walk out of the bedroom, back into the living room, and walk over to the large window gazing down on the world.

"You this bossy in the sack, too, tesoro?" Dante calls from the bedroom, but I hear him pick up the cordless phone.

It will be fine. They'll give us another room, no biggie.

Dante's low timbre sounds from the bedroom, but I can't make out what he's saying. A couple of minutes later, he joins me in the living room, but I don't turn around.

"We're stuck with this one. No other rooms."

I turn around and narrow my eyes at Dante. "You did this on purpose!"

He raises both hands. "You sure think highly of yourself."

"There's no other explanation."

"My father," he says. "He had the room booked."

That makes a lot more sense, and I suddenly feel really stupid.

"If you can't handle being close . . ." He smirks.

My hands fist at my sides. There's no way I'm letting him think he can get to me more than he already has.

"It's fine," I bite out.

"You sure? You look—"

"I said it's fine. It's a big bed."

A knock sounds on the door of the suite, and I figure it must be our bags we left with the porter. I go to answer it, but Dante rushes ahead, beating me to the door. He throws his arm against my stomach, pushing me behind him as he looks through the peephole, his hand moving to the back of his pants. He's got a gun on him.

He takes the bags from the bellhop and tips him before shutting and locking the door. "You don't ever answer the door. Especially without looking first, but just . . . I open the door if we don't have security." His jaw clenches as he bears down on me.

"I'm going to have a shower, then I'm going to bed. Right side is mine." I head into the bathroom and slam the door.

* * *

LUCKILY, I FELL asleep quickly after my head hit the pillow last night. Which means I was in bed alone since Dante was still out in the living room, doing whatever he does. Watching some sporting event by the sounds of it.

I'm honestly not sure if I'd have been able to fall asleep if he'd been in bed with me, and that bothers me. Because my lack of sleep wouldn't have been about being worried he was going to smother me, but more from the awareness he was only a couple of feet away. The sound of his breath in the dark room and the scent of him so close.

I give my head a shake as I finish perfecting my hair before we leave. I'm dressed in a pair of black high-waisted dress pants and a thin gray cashmere bodysuit with long sleeves, hair down in waves. I pair it with my black Louboutin pumps, and I'm ready to go.

"Car's downstairs," Dante announces, appearing in the doorway to the en suite.

"I'm ready." I turn and walk over to the doorway, but Dante doesn't budge. "You'll need to move if we plan on leaving."

He blinks a couple of times then backs away so I can squeeze past him. "Yeah, about fucking time."

That was weird.

Heading to the closet near the entry, I grab my long wool coat and slide it on, do up the buttons, and grab my purse. Dante is as handsome as ever, I begrudgingly admit. He's wearing a tailored black suit, white shirt, and red tie. It fits his body perfectly, showing off his muscled physique.

"Let's go." I turn and open the door, but he slams it shut with his hand. I draw back.

"What did I tell you last night?" he seethes.

"No one is there," I say.

"That you know of. Are you sure you're a Bratva princess?" He opens the door and peers both ways, then takes my hand and steps out.

We make our way down the elevator, through the lobby, and out onto the sidewalk with his large manly hand around mine. We probably appear like a couple. When we're a few steps away from the SUV, a loud bang rings out, and I'm flattened to the pavement.

"What the hell!" I shout.

Dante is on top of me, looking around, up and down the sidewalk, eyes wide and alert. He can't see the street itself because of the vehicle in front of us. Finally, he looks down at me.

"Are you okay?" His gaze traces the lines of my face and down my body as if I've been shot.

"Besides being sacked like a quarterback, I'm great." I push at his shoulders to get him off of me, but he doesn't budge.

I realize then that he assumed the sound was a gunshot. Oh no . . . he thought it was a gunshot, and he . . . tried to protect me. No. The idea of it confuses me. He doesn't want to be tied to me any more than I want to be tied to him. Wouldn't he be happy if someone tried to take me out?

"It was a car backfiring. Do they not have those in California?" I push at his shoulders once again, and he scowls at me.

"Most people say thank you when you try to save their life. Next time I won't bother."

Our driver, Aleks, rushes around the SUV. "Are you all right, Polina?"

Dante rolls off me and gets himself up. Aleks puts out a hand for me, but Dante steps in front of him, as if demanding I accept his.

"I'm fine." I bend and brush off the back of my coat and lift my feet to check the back of my pants. My idiot fiancé is lucky he didn't rip anything.

By the time I'm satisfied I don't need to go back up and change, Dante is stewing, I can tell. Anger is wafting off him in waves. I don't know why he's pissed. I'm the one who was tackled to the ground.

But as Aleks drives us nearer and nearer to my family's brownstone, I feel bad, which is a foreign feeling for me.

"Thank you," I say quietly. I think I say it so quietly that I'm almost hoping he doesn't hear it.

But he must, because he turns his head from gazing out the window to look at me on the seat beside him. "One thing you should know about me . . . I may not want this marriage any more than you do, but I take care of what's mine. For better or worse, you're mine now, and I'll do what I have to in order to protect you, even if it means tackling you to the ground on a dirty New York street."

Stupid tears burn in my eyes. It's not like I'm not used to being under protection. Maybe it's because he's the first person to take ownership of my protection. Maybe because I'm used to the person who's supposed to protect me hurting me.

"The streets aren't that dirty," I say, unable to deal with the intimacy of what he said and wanting to change the conversation.

"Please." He guffaws. "This city is a cesspit. Wait until you live in California for a few months. You'll probably hate coming back here."

For the first time, I realize that New York won't be my home anymore. After we marry, I'll have to live with him in California. I may look more like a California girl on the outside, but inside, I'm all New York.

There's no way I'll fit in there. Just another crappy thing to go along with this engagement.

CHAPTER NINE

DANTE

Our meal consisted of what Polina told me were some pretty common Russian dishes like gherkins, pickled mushrooms, meat pies, and sauerkraut. I've never missed Italian food more.

So far I've kept to myself and not really spoken to anyone. Everyone—what has to be fifty of them—turned and stared at us in silence when Polina and I walked into the house. Tension in the brownstone is high, to say the least.

I was patted down when I arrived, but I'm sure no one else was. I knew one of their family would be driving us to and from the gathering, and I prayed that Dmitri had his guys in line by now so they don't go rogue and kill me. So I'm very aware that one word from me and any one of these stronzos could whip out their guns and put me underground, and I'd have no defense.

I stand in the back of the room, leaning against the wall, sipping on my drink and observing Polina. I'll give it to the Russians—they know their vodka.

The mask she's perfected remains in place as she flits around the room. She's clearly more comfortable in this environment with the people she knows well and probably grew up with. I've caught moments where her façade slips, but she's quick to realize it and put it back on display.

"You will have your hands full with her." Nikita, Polina's mother, sidles up beside me.

"Tell me something I don't know." I give her a wry smile before downing the last of my vodka on ice.

"It doesn't seem like it, but deep down, she's sensitive."

I bite my cheek to stop from laughing. "Not sure that's how I'd describe her." I don't turn in Nikita's direction, which would be rude in most circumstances, but I have to watch my back from all sides tonight.

Pavel goes over to Polina, who is standing with her friends Irina and Oksana, and says something in her ear. Her smile fades, and she stiffens, instantly losing that mask.

My forehead wrinkles. There's something off about her when she's around him. I noticed it when she was at my house before Christmas, too.

Nikita's hand lands on my forearm, drawing my attention away from her daughter. "That's what she wants you to think. Everyone." She gestures around the room at everyone gathered there. "But it's not who she really is."

I nod. "I'll have to take your word for it."

"Please be good to her."

Hearing the worry in her voice, I face her, and her eyes say the same thing as her tone. A mother's worry that her daughter's been promised to the enemy. I'm not sure it's ever been done in our worlds, and she has every reason to be as worried as she appears.

I sigh, putting myself in her shoes if Polina were my little sister, Lucia. I would want the same for her, so I decide to be as honest as I can. "Listen, I'm not going to tell you that I want this union and that I'm happy about it, because we both know I'd be lying. But I can promise you that I will provide for her. And I'll never raise a hand to her. She will be well cared for. Most importantly, I will protect her."

Sadly, the only thing I can't tell her mom is that she'll be loved, which isn't uncommon in my family.

"Those are all wonderful things, but they aren't love." Nikita glances at her daughter and frowns. Then she walks away before I have an opportunity to say anything that might appease her.

Polina looks at me at that moment and holds my stare.

I wish I could love her, of course I do. It would make both of our lives easier and more fulfilled, but that's never going to happen. In my eyes, she'll always be the enemy.

* * *

BY THE TIME the night wraps up and we're leaving, Polina has clearly had too much to drink. I'm surprised because she seems to value control over her emotions and actions. Being as I've been surrounded by enemies, I only sipped on two drinks all night.

"Did you enjoy yourself?" I ask her in the back of the SUV on the way back to the hotel.

She's sprawled out on the opposite side of the seat, her head pressed against the leather and turned toward the window. She rolls her head around in my direction, not bothering to lift it from the seat. "Sure. As much fun as I can have when everyone is watching my every move to see how I'm acting toward you."

We didn't put on the display of a happy couple, but we were cordial enough. For the most part, I stood away from everyone while she made the rounds.

"Did you have fun?" she asks, the words all melding together in one big slur.

I chuckle. "As much fun as one can have when they're surrounded by people who want you dead, all speaking a language you don't understand."

She laughs, holding her stomach and squeezing her eyes shut.

I've never seen her like this. It's a little jarring to see her so . . . carefree. It's a good version of her, and I have the brief thought that if this is who she really is, our marriage could be a lot easier.

She notices my attention on her, and her laughter stops abruptly. "What?"

I shrug. "I've just never seen you like this."

Polina lets out a short bark of laughter. "You don't even know me."

Truth. I've spent hardly any time with her since our engagement was announced.

"Maybe we should rectify that." I'm curious about her now that her guard is down.

She eyes me like maybe she doesn't trust me or the words coming out of my mouth. She'd be smart not to.

"Okay, you first," she says as though it's a challenge.

"All right, what do you want to know?"

Polina ponders it for a minute before she asks her question. "Why do you sleep with so many women?"

I laugh. "That's what you want to know?"

She shrugs.

"All right . . ." It's not something I've ever given any thought to, so I take a moment to form my response. She keeps her expectant gaze on me the entire time I consider her question. "Sometimes I'm bored, and there's nothing else to do. Sometimes I'm stressed, and I need a way to release that stress. Other times I enjoy pleasure—both giving and receiving."

I don't miss the way her thighs clench together at my last statement.

"Have you ever been faithful to a woman?" she asks.

I arch an eyebrow. "Are you concerned about my fidelity during our marriage?"

She scowls. "I don't care what you do."

"Really?"

"Really." She locks her gaze with mine as if in a challenge.

I slide over until we're shoulder to shoulder, thigh to thigh. I set my hand on her knee and squeeze. "So you wouldn't mind if I used my fingers to pleasure another woman . . ." My hand trails farther up her leg until it's almost at the juncture of her thighs.

"Nope." Her voice is barely a whisper.

"And if I used my tongue to pleasure another woman . . ." I sweep back the blond locks hanging over her shoulder. "You'd be okay with that, too?" Leaning in, I swipe my tongue up the column of her neck.

She shivers, and I watch as her nipples pebble under her tight top.

Thank God she refused to put on her coat when we were leaving, otherwise I wouldn't get this mouthwatering view of her tits.

"And what about my cock?" I lightly bite her earlobe, and a small moan erupts from her throat, so quiet I almost miss it. "Would it be okay if my cock made another woman come?"

Taking her hand, I place it on the rigid length currently trying to poke out of my pants. I'm taking my chances. She could very well punch me there, but she squeezes it in her palm, making me moan. She squeezes it again, and I fight to keep my eyes open.

"You haven't answered my question." My voice is low and gravelly.

Polina slowly turns her head to face me, and when our blue eyes meet, I see white-hot flames of desire in hers. She may hate me, but she wants to fuck me.

I'd never deny her a hate fuck.

So I lean in, lest she change her mind and decide to rip my cock off rather than what she's doing to it now, squeezing and rubbing. I'm not even entirely sure she knows what she's doing.

When she doesn't balk, my lips fall to hers, tentative at first. The pillowy softness of her lips settles in, and my body heats with a demand that I take her. Still, I force myself to ease her into the idea of kissing me. Once, twice, three times, I bring my lips to hers in short kisses until I lick the seam of her lips.

She opens her mouth for me, and when our tongues touch for the first time and I taste her, I'm holding on by a thin thread. Lust roars like a furnace, heating my blood. My fingers tangle in her hair, and I deepen the kiss.

Polina moans into my mouth, shifting to straddle me in the back seat and threading her hands into my hair. The warmth between her spread thighs rocks against the hard length between my legs. I nip on her plump bottom lip as the SUV comes to a stop. I pull back far enough to look at her.

"Take me to our room," she says.

I debate this in my head and not because I don't want to. She's got me more turned on than I've ever been. But maybe this is going too fast. I can't disappear on her tomorrow. Polina's my fiancée. Plus, she's clearly been drinking. Yes, eventually we're going to sleep together, but we'll just be doing it to extend the bloodline.

If I sleep with her now, it will be because I want to. I'll be taking her for myself. And it's hard not to feel as if that's a betrayal of everything I was raised to believe, even if my father is asking me to do a one-eighty.

I stare at her for a beat, contemplating, my thumb running along her bottom lip.

"Please," she whispers and grinds down onto my dick.

I'm too weak of a man to say no.

The driver opens the door, and Polina doesn't move, so I shift myself to the edge of the seat and somehow manage to step out of the car with her legs and arms around me. The driver tries to hand me her coat.

"Leave it with the front desk," I tell him and walk into the hotel, the doorman opening the door for me.

Polina kisses my neck as I carry her across the lobby, and my dick hardens further. I try to smile at the people we're passing as if there's nothing to see here, but truthfully, they're staring at a couple who is going to fuck like crazy when they get up to their room.

Our lips join again while we wait for the elevator, and when it dings, I pull back enough to see where we're going. She rests her head on my shoulder as I press the button for our floor, and the elevator rises.

When I reach our room, I fumble for the key in my pocket, but eventually I get it and open the door. I lock the door and waste no time walking straight to the bedroom, where I lean over to gently lay Polina on the mattress. I'm about to instruct her to get naked, but when I pull back, she's asleep—or probably more accurately, passed out.

Pushing my hands through my hair, I sigh, then glance at the erection tenting my pants.

Probably for the best anyway. There's no doubt I would have regretted it come morning.

Polina is still in her dress pants and tight body suit, but I know she'll feel violated if I remove her clothes, as uncomfortable as they'll be to sleep, and probably wake up, in, so I simply remove the heels she's wearing, admiring the arch of her foot and her pale pink–painted toes. When I shift her body so that I can pull the covers from under her, she doesn't even stir. I pull them up over her body and retreat to the bathroom to take care of myself.

There will be no sleep for me until the scent of her is off of me, and I rub one out to the thought of what could have happened tonight.

CHAPTER TEN
POLINA

There's a dull throbbing ache in my head. My mouth is dry and pasty. The heat of bare skin pressed against my cheek registers, and my eyes spring open.

"Easy there," Dante's deep rumble sounds in my ear, and I feel the weight of his arm around my back.

Oh my god. I'm sprawled over him in the hotel bed.

Did we—nope. I rub my legs together and feel I'm still clothed. Thank god.

"What the hell?" I push myself off his hard chest, trying not to notice how muscled it is.

He grins at me, hair perfectly mussed, bare-chested as if he just stepped out of a magazine. "You were like a toddler, and I was your favorite stuffed animal all night. Didn't have the heart to push you away after the third time."

My face heats with embarrassment. How much did I drink last night? The end of the evening is murky, the memories hazy around the edges and disjointed. I recall drinking more than I usually would because of all the attention on us and the way it felt as if people were judging me as a traitor for being engaged to Dante, even though I had nothing to do with the decision.

Then it was time to leave, and on the drive home . . .

Dante's laugh echoes throughout the quiet room. "Remembering how you jumped me last night?"

"I did not jump you," I hiss.

"Offered yourself to me? Is that a better phrasing?" He arches an eyebrow. "Take me to our room," he says in a high-pitched girly voice clearly meant to mock me.

"I was drunk. It wouldn't have mattered who I was with." It's a lie. We both know it's a lie.

"Keep telling yourself that."

My face grows even hotter, which I wouldn't have thought possible. Aggravated, I whip off the covers and stomp toward the bathroom. "I'm having a shower before we leave."

His annoying laugh fills the room, and I slam the door.

* * *

ONCE AGAIN, WE travel back to Sicuro on his family's private plane while my brothers and friends use our jet. When I called Dmitri this morning and begged him to let me travel with them, he shut me down.

Before taking over as the head of the Bratva when Feliks died, he could be reasoned with. He was understanding. But I see that changing. His priorities have shifted from my happiness to what's best for the family, and I can't help but feel betrayed on some level. He used to be the one who looked out for me.

"You want to pick up where we left off last night?" Dante nods toward the bedroom at the back of the plane. He has that stupid cocky grin I'd love to slap off him like I did during the party.

"You wish." I glare.

"You're right. I quite enjoyed how you threw yourself at me and rubbed all over me like a cat in heat, like a . . . wait. I looked it up on Google Translate this morning . . . my kotik."

Fury roars to life inside my chest. "I am not your kitten."

He leans forward, forearms draped over his knees. "Not yet."

"Never."

"Do Russians not know the saying 'Never say never,' tesoro?"

"Some things are certain."

He leans back and looks down his nose at me, widening the opening of his legs. "Maybe. But not this."

He looks like a snack, and a goddamn delicious one. Legs spread wide to match his wide shoulders, all power and strength. His pale blue eyes don't budge from me as I challenge his gaze.

Maybe it wouldn't be so bad to sleep with him. Eventually, I'm going to.

No! What am I thinking? I cannot let him wear me down. He may not have pulled the trigger that killed my brother, but he played a role in it. He was there that day.

I don't know what, but I'm going to have to do something. Something drastic. Because I cannot allow myself to fall for Dante. Only an idiot asking to be hurt would fall for their enemy. I can't trust him. I can't *ever* trust him, and I need to remember that.

And I'm not going to marry him. I'll never fit in by his side, and I'll be ostracized from my own people. I heard all the whispers behind my back at our Christmas celebration when I arrived with him. It's a miracle that nothing happened to set off either side.

"We'll see," I say, determined to figure out something. "Now be quiet. I want to sleep off my hangover."

* * *

I STEP INTO Moskva House and know right away that something is up. Everyone is looking at me and whispering. Not everyone has returned from their Orthodox Christmas celebrations yet, but there are enough people to make it obvious it's me who's garnered their interest.

What the hell?

I spot Sasha talking to one of his friends, and I make my way over to him. He smiles when he sees me, but it doesn't reach his eyes.

"Hey, how was your celebration with your family?" I ask.

"Good. Just got back a couple of hours ago."

I nod in the direction away from his friend, and he follows when I step to the side. I lean in. "Why do I feel like everyone is looking at me strangely?"

He clears his throat and averts his eyes. "They heard about New York."

My forehead wrinkles. "That I was forced to bring Dante along with me?"

Sasha shakes his head and frowns, as if it's taking everything in him to tell me. "That you were wrapped around him when you went up to your hotel room Saturday night."

I blanche. Stupid Aleks and his big fucking mouth. My brother will be hearing about this. "That's not . . . I mean, I was drunk. He was just carrying me up to my room."

Sasha crosses his arms. "That's not how I heard it."

As usual, when I'm backed into a corner, my claws come out. "Well, I don't care what you heard, that's the truth." Sort of. Not really.

This is exactly why I cannot fall for Dante. Cannot marry him unless I want to be ostracized by everyone. It's not working. This little plan is a failed experiment, and I'm going to be the one who pays the price.

"So you're not into him?" He studies my face.

I shake my head, imploring him to believe me, even though I don't even know if I believe myself. "No, I swear."

Just then, someone walks up behind me and says under their breath, "Dante already stuffing that Italian sausage into you?"

My jaw clenches, and my breath picks up while I pretend I didn't hear it. But Sasha doesn't take the same approach. He pushes past me, and when I whirl around, he's tugging one of the guys from the Vasiliev family toward him by the shirt.

"You have something to say?" Sasha says, right up in his face.

"Fuck off." He pushes at Sasha's hands, which doesn't dislodge Sasha from him.

"Apologize to Polina," Sasha says between gritted teeth. "Now!"

The Vasiliev guy seems to size up Sasha then glances around. I have to assume that the only reason he looks in my direction and says a quiet sorry is because he's outnumbered. There are more Aminoffs here than Vasilievs.

I nod, just wanting Sasha to let him go. It's only drawing more attention to me.

Sasha pushes him away so hard that the guy stumbles backward and almost lands on his ass.

After the guy walks away, I say to Sasha, "You didn't have to do that."

He glowers at me. "He can't talk about you like that without any consequences."

"Well, thank you." I squeeze his forearm.

I don't miss the way Sasha clocks the movement and how his tongue darts out to lick his lips.

And that sparks an idea for how I might get myself out of this whole mess.

CHAPTER ELEVEN
DANTE

The moment I step into Roma House, Gabriele Vitale spots me from where he sits beside his wife, Aria Costa, in the lounge. He's now the head of the Vitale crime family, which runs the northwest portion of the country. His father was killed by the Russians a couple of months back, which was a big part of what set off this war between the two sides.

"Wasn't sure whether we'd see you walk back in here." Gabriele gets up and approaches.

"Disappointed?" I arch an eyebrow.

Of all the other heads of the crime families or next-in-lines like myself, I get along best with Gabriele. Marcelo and I always butt heads because the guy is a prick. Antonio and I get along well enough, but he's Marcelo's brother-in-law, so I wouldn't tell him anything I didn't want getting back to Marcelo.

"Not at all. The last thing I'd want is you out of the way so your little brother could take over one day."

I chuckle. Obviously, Gabriele's still pissed that my brother had an interest in Aria before he and she were an official item.

"You and me both." I shove my hands in my pockets.

"So everything went well?" he asks, seeming a little skeptical.

"As well as you'd anticipate. They weren't happy I was there, nor was I." I shrug. "Wait. How did you even know where I'd been?"

Gabriele gives me a sly grin. "Word travels."

"Yeah, or you and your computer shit are spying on people." I frown.

Gabriele's a huge computer nerd and has his surveillance equipment smuggled into the school every year, then he barters information for favors.

"Not at all. It's big news when one of us spends the weekend with our enemies."

I blow out a breath and push a hand through my hair. "No shit. Imagine the gossip when we actually get married."

"How are you feeling about that?" He studies me.

It occurs to me that he might be the first person who has asked me that. "Not pleased. How do you think?"

"Wasn't sure, given that I heard that you carried Polina through the lobby of your hotel while she was wrapped around you."

"Word really does travel fast, huh?"

"It's big news."

"She was hammered. It's not what you think."

It is what he thinks, but I don't know why I don't admit it. I could belittle Polina for hitting on me when she was drunk and use it to my advantage. It's one thing to get a rise out of her and irritate her, but it's another to let others be privy to what happened between us that night.

"Sure, it's not." The knowing grin on Gabriele's face irks me.

Before I can tell him to watch himself, my brother and Santino join us. Gabriele returns to Aria on the couch, and I'm forced to give them the same rundown I just gave to Gabriele. They're in disbelief that nothing popped off between the Russians and me.

"I kept my mouth shut. I may be impulsive, but I'm not an idiot. I know when I'm outnumbered," I say.

"I didn't think you had it in you," Dom says, patting my shoulder.

I shrug off his touch. "Had what?"

"The ability to shut the fuck up when it's in your best interest."

My eyes narrow. "Watch it, little brother."

He laughs.

"Your fiancée getting any closer to accepting this marriage?" Santino asks.

I laugh. "Fuck no. Still the same cold bitch she always is."

For some reason, the words taste sour.

"You've got your hands full with that one," Santino says.

Not wanting to continue this conversation, I try to lighten the mood so we can move on. "You're telling me." I raise my hands and motion as if I'm squeezing a pair of breasts.

"Speaking of big tits," Dom says, "Isabelle has been roaming around here, waiting for you to show up."

A couple of weeks ago, that news would have made me happy. I would have gone in search of her, brought her to my room, and fucked her to take the edge off. But it doesn't sound as appealing now.

Why does the mention of Isabelle sound like one more problem I have to deal with, rather than an opportunity to make my problems go away?

"Thanks for the warning. I'll see you guys later." Without waiting for a response, I take off toward the elevator and retreat to my room.

I've only been chilling in here for about twenty minutes when there's a knock at the door. I don't even have to open it to know who it is. I know, thanks to my brother's warning.

I swing the door open, and Isabelle stands there, a coy smile in place.

"Glad to see you made it back in one piece. I thought you might be wearing concrete shoes at the bottom of the Hudson by now."

"Still breathing, as you can see." I motion down the length of my body.

"Maybe I should do a closer inspection to make sure everything's in order." She steps toward me and places her hand on my chest, pushing her giant tits against me.

Usually by now my dick would be stirring, showing some interest . . . but nothing. What the fuck?

I chuckle. "I can assure you, all parts of me are working just fine." I would know. I had to rub one out twice last night before bed after Polina left me with blue balls.

"You can never be too sure." She trails her hand down my chest until she reaches between my legs, then frowns when she doesn't find me erect. She tries to play it off like she doesn't care. "Not in the mood?"

"Just tired. Had to sleep with one eye open all weekend, you know?"

She gives me a bit of a sad smile. "Oh well, do you want to hang out then?" She takes a step forward into my room, but I put a hand on her shoulder.

"Not really in the mood for that either."

She holds my stare for a beat then nods, jutting her chin into the air. "Fine, but one day you'll want me back, and I won't be there."

I watch her walk down to the elevator, then I go back into my room and close the door. I push my hands into my hair and stand there for a minute, contemplating what the fuck is wrong with me. I just turned down an attractive, willing woman. I can't remember the last time I did that. Not sure I ever have.

All this shit with Polina is getting to me. That must be it. It was a long weekend, and I was on edge for a lot of it, given my surroundings. I just need to get back into my regular routine, and then I'll be fine, and I'll want to titty-fuck Isabelle by this time tomorrow. I know it.

CHAPTER TWELVE
POLINA

Tonight is when I'll enact the first part of my plan to escape this engagement.

I tug down the thin V-neck cashmere sweater I'm wearing with jeans, just to show a little more cleavage. My makeup is a little heavier than I normally wear, and I make sure to put on my knee-high black boots with my skinny jeans. All things I know Sasha loves.

I've asked him to meet me at Café Ambrosia. He's going to help me with some of my schoolwork for my embezzlement class. He's a year older, so he's already taken the class. I'm not really having trouble with it, but I need a reason to spend time with him in public where people won't be whispering rumors that might get back to Dante—or worse, my brothers.

Once I'm satisfied with my appearance, I head out of my room and over to the café.

Sasha is already there when I arrive, and he smiles and waves at me. My plan isn't a particularly sophisticated one. It's something I saw on a true crime show once. Basically, I plan to coax Sasha into killing Dante. How? By withholding what he wants most, but giving him the idea that he can have it if Dante were out of the way. It's not something I can achieve overnight, but over time, I think I can do it.

I could kill Dante myself, sure. But I don't have the stomach for it. Even though I was born into this life and am no stranger to death, I could never kill someone. There's enough guilt gnawing at me from the idea of coaxing Sasha into killing Dante, never mind taking his life myself. But I cannot be forced to marry Dante and spend my life with him. It will feel like a jail sentence being married to a man who hates me, surrounded by people who hate me and will likely resent any children I bear.

So this is my best shot, since all my arguments are falling on deaf ears with Dmitri.

I push aside the guilt and smile and walk toward the table. "Hey, thanks again for meeting me."

I come to a stop a few steps from the table, allowing Sasha to give me the once-over, his gaze snagging on the V of my sweater and on my boots.

"Hey, no problem at all. Happy to help." He motions for me to sit, and I do. "Did you want something to drink before we start?"

"I'd love a hot chocolate with whipped cream."

He chuckles. "A hot chocolate? That's cute." Then he pushes his chair out from the table and stands.

"What? It's cold out." My most flirtatious giggle falls flawlessly from my mouth. But I'm not the giddy schoolgirl type, and he knows that. Maybe I'm laying it on too thick.

"Be right back."

While he's gone getting us drinks, I pull my textbook from my bag, along with my notebook and pens. We're not allowed any laptops on campus—too much of a security risk apparently—and the only computers we have access to are in the computer lab. So good old-fashioned textbooks it is.

"Here you go." Sasha slides the hot chocolate in front of me.

"Thanks."

We go through some things, and I pretend I don't understand, something that rankles, but it's clear that Sasha likes thinking I need him, so I keep up the act.

About ten minutes in, I look at him. "Why don't you bring your chair over here beside me so we're on the same side of the table? Then we don't have to keep turning the textbook back and forth between us."

This feels like something I can get away with in public. It makes sense that we'd sit side-by-side.

Without protest, he brings his chair over to my side. We're sitting at a table designed for two people, so I shift slightly to the left, and he comes to sit at my right, so close that our shoulders and thighs are practically touching.

"That's better." I look to my right and meet his gaze, forcing myself to hold it.

"Definitely." He smiles widely.

I slide my tongue out of my mouth, slowly licking my bottom lip. He watches with rapt attention. I break eye contact first—can't be too obvious—and we get back to work.

After another couple of minutes, I deemed it finally time to drink my hot chocolate. It was boiling hot when I got it, but it should be cool enough to enjoy now. I bring the mug to my lips and take a small sip.

I moan, purposefully adding a sexual undertone to the sound. "It's so good."

Sasha's eyelids are heavy when I peek at him.

"You have something . . ." He points at my upper lip. "May I?"

"Of course," I say in a breathy voice I don't actually feel.

He swipes over my lip with his thumb. I push back the thought of how it doesn't feel anything like when Dante ran his thumb over my lips this weekend. "You had a bit of whipped cream there."

"Thanks." I dip my tongue out and trace the path he just took with his thumb.

Then we get back to work. It's probably best to keep him guessing at first—was I really showing signs of interest, or is he reading into things? Let his emotions bounce all over the place.

So for the next hour, I don't flirt at all. I focus on what we're seemingly here for and take notes on the things he's explaining, do a few practice problems, and once it feels as though we've been here long enough, I shut the textbook.

"I think if we do any more tonight, my brain will explode." I look at him as if I'm a helpless female in need of guidance.

Already I feel myself softening toward Dante, being drawn to him, and I cannot trust that or myself. It will only end in my own destruction. He wouldn't be the first guy I thought would protect me but ended up hurting me.

"You did great. Once I explained things, you caught on really quickly." He squeezes my hand as though I'm a child in need of praise.

I have to physically bite my tongue to keep myself from saying something to the contrary.

"Do you think you'll need my help again?" His voice sounds almost hopeful.

I give him a small smile. "If you're willing and offering."

"Of course. Anything you need, just ask."

I hope he means that. I really do.

A sad smile emerges on my face. "I wish it were that easy." I tuck my hands onto my lap and look down at them.

"What's wrong?" The worry is evident in his voice.

"Nothing." Raising my head, I meet his eyes and give what is obviously a fake smile.

"That's not true, I can tell." His head tilts, assessing.

I turn and face him, my knees touching the side of his thigh, and place my left hand on the table. "It's nothing. I . . . I shouldn't talk about it."

His eyebrows furrow. "We've known each other a long time. You can talk to me about anything."

My stomach roils. Am I really going to do this? Because this next step will cross over into what is very much a lie. A lie designed for my own gain.

I'm not ignorant of what people think of me. Everyone assumes I'm a cold-hearted bitch devoid of feeling. It's my own fault. That's how I present myself to the world, but it's just what I use to keep people at a distance, to keep myself from trusting the wrong person and ending up devastated.

That's what propels me forward—the idea of doing it again with Dante. A man I know is my sworn enemy, but who I find myself intrigued by, turned on by, who's piqued my interest. I can't allow myself to continue down that path. I have to do whatever it takes to divert my future away from him, and the only way to do that is for him to no longer exist.

And so, I tell the lie.

"I know," I say in a quiet voice. "I was interested in you, too, but I was scared."

He frowns. "Why would you be scared?"

I look away from him, as though I'm too shy to say the words and continue our eye contact. "Because of how much I felt for you. And now . . . now it's too late."

He sighs, and I look back at him. "Dmitri won't budge on this marriage?"

Shaking my head, I bite my bottom lip. "No, and Dante . . . he, he scares me."

The words taste like poison because while they're the truth, he scares me in a much different way than physical harm.

Sasha places his hand on top of mine on the table. We hold eye contact in silence for several beats, and then a shadow falls over the table.

I couldn't have planned it better myself. Dante stands beside our table, staring at us with rage-filled eyes.

CHAPTER THIRTEEN
DANTE

I'm just finishing my workout when my school-issued cell phone rings. I glance down and see Dmitri Aminoff's name on my screen.

What the fuck does he want?

"Yeah?" I answer.

"You and Polina need to do better. Have her sit at your table for dinner tomorrow night."

"You might be *a* Bratva boss, Dmitri, but you're not my boss. You'd do well to remember that."

He chuckles. "We discussed this at your house before Christmas. Your father agrees."

I bite back a curse because he's right. My father forced me to go spend the weekend with her family right in the heart of enemy territory. He'd think nothing of Polina sitting at the Accardi table in the dining hall.

I pass Antonio and Sofia La Rosa, hand in hand on the path back to Roma House, and lift my chin in greeting. Fucking lovebirds. It's ridiculous. The cold air bites at the exposed skin on my face and hands as I walk down the stone path.

"Polina will never go for it." There, I've made it his problem.

"She will. And if she doesn't, tell me, and I'll deal with her."

Months ago, the idea of getting Polina in trouble with her brother probably would have made me gleeful, but for whatever reason, it doesn't anymore.

I mutter another curse. "I'll deal with her. She's going to have to get used to taking my orders at some point anyway, since we're going to be married." I add the last sentence to cover the real reason I don't want her in shit with Dmitri.

"Good. Irina told me she was studying in the café tonight," he says and hangs up.

"Stronzo." I shove my phone back in my pocket.

Since I'm already halfway to Roma House, I decide to drop off my gym bag, then head back out to the café to track down Polina and tell her the good news.

I think I still have a bottle of whiskey stashed in my room. Maybe I'll take a shot before I head out. This news is sure to start an argument.

* * *

I STEP INTO the café and look around for Polina.

I'm assuming I'll find her with her friends at one of the tables, books splayed in front of them, but instead she's at a table with some Russian prick whose name I don't know, but he's the asshole she was all over at the party. And don't they look fucking cozy now? He even has his hand over hers.

My jaw set, I stalk over to the table, deciding not to say a word and just stand there to see how long it takes them to notice me.

Too fucking long for my liking.

I stare at them, rage boiling—for what reason, I'm not even exactly sure—until Polina glances up. She startles, eyes wide when she sees me.

"What are you doing here?" she asks in a voice that's both frightened and unsure. Two emotions I've never once heard from this woman's mouth.

My eyes narrow. "I think the better question is, what are you doing?" I glance at the piece of shit sitting beside her who is sizing me up.

Polina slips her hand out from under his and places it in her lap. "Sasha is helping me with one of my classes."

"Sasha needs to leave." I don't bother diverting my eyes from her to him.

He stands and steps over to me. It's almost laughable. I think he's trying to intimidate me, but he's shorter than me and not quite as strong. Wouldn't matter if he were a foot taller and a bodybuilder, though. I wouldn't back down.

It's no secret to anyone that this is an arranged marriage, but we're supposed to be showing that we can come together, that once we got to know each other, we fell for one another. But pretending that's why I'm pissed about this whole situation is bullshit, and I know it.

I'm pissed because this guy thinks he can swoop in and try to take what's mine by right, and there won't be any consequences.

"We have a problem, Sasha?" I raise an eyebrow and step forward.

At this moment, I don't give a shit about the no-violence rule. If Sasha needs a lesson about the appropriate way to act around someone else's fiancée, I'm happy to be the one to give it to him.

"No problem. We were just finishing up, weren't we, Sasha?" Polina says in a somewhat pleading voice.

He looks away from me—stupid move that's going to get him killed one day—and looks at her. Polina looks up at him, brilliant blue eyes full of concern—for him, I think—and without a word, he walks away from the table.

"Good decision," I say to his back and see him tense, but he keeps walking.

"Do you have to be such a caveman?" Polina snipes, all traces of the weak little fawn she was moments ago gone.

I slip into the seat Sasha vacated and lean in over her until her back is bowed against the arm of her chair. "What the fuck did I just walk in on?"

"A friend helping me with my studies. What's the big deal?" She glares.

"You two looked pretty cozy."

She rolls her eyes. "Are you always this jealous?" A cruel little smirk rests on her face. "Or is it just with me? Who would have thought . . . Dante the manwhore is actually jealous." She arches an eyebrow, daring me to deny it.

I give her a sly grin of my own. "It has nothing to do with you, tesoro, so don't get your hopes up. I just don't like another man thinking he can take what's mine."

"I'm not yours," she says between gritted teeth.

A deep chuckle sounds in my chest. "That's where you're wrong. You're wearing *my* ring. You will be *my* wife in mere months. Like it or not, you're *mine*." I back away, allowing her to sit straight up.

She sucks in a breath, and I don't miss the way she ever so slightly pushes her thighs together.

I hum, low in my throat. "That pussy gets all wet when I'm possessive, huh?"

"You're such a pig."

I laugh as she gathers her things from the tabletop, shoving them into her bag.

"Stay away from him."

Her head whips in my direction. "I'm allowed to have friends."

"*Female* friends."

"I'll be friends with whoever I want, Dante." She pushes away from the table and slings her bag over her shoulder.

I stand, too, forcing her to crane her neck to look up at me since I'm so much taller. "Push me, and see what happens." My tone is a warning.

She must sense it because I see real fear in her eyes then. It makes me feel as if a tight band is winding around my chest.

"How did you even find me?" she asks.

"Irina told your brother you were studying in the café."

She grinds her teeth. "Remind me to thank her later."

"You weren't exactly hard to find. Out here flirting with that piece of shit for anyone to see."

"I'm not defending myself to you." She pushes past me to leave, but I grab hold of her arm, forcing her to turn around.

"I came here for a reason."

She yanks her arm from my hold. "Then say it, and leave me alone. I've had enough of you already."

"Aw, you'll never have enough of me once you've had me." I wink, just to piss her off.

It works. The pale, creamy skin on her face turns a deep pink. "What do you want?"

"You're going to eat at the Accardi table for dinner tomorrow night. Brother's orders."

Her shoulders fall. "Why would I do that?"

I shrug. "Keeping up appearances and all that." She opens her mouth to say something, but I cut her off. "Don't bother arguing. It's happening. I'll pick you up outside Moskva House at five thirty. Don't make me wait."

I'm the one to leave first, just because it will rile her up, and I like a riled-up Polina.

CHAPTER FOURTEEN
POLINA

Once more, I begged Dmitri not to make me do this—eat with the Italians—to no avail. He wouldn't budge. It makes me so angry and makes me feel so alone.

I stand outside the Moskva House, waiting for Dante to appear. My *Italian* fiancé.

What's everyone going to think when they see me sitting at his table? I doubt anyone will even speak to me at all. It will be the world's most awkward dinner.

I don't know how Dante did Christmas at my place. I don't think I'll be able to handle one dinner, let alone an entire day and night.

I don't have to wait long. Dante strolls up the path. The sun has just dipped below the horizon since it's January, but the lights lining the path bounce off the natural blond highlights in his light brown hair. I recognize his gait, too. He walks with this strange mix of intensity coupled with a laissez-faire attitude. As though he has no worries in the world, but if something were to pop up, he has every confidence he can handle it.

When his face comes into view, it's clear to me that he's looking forward to this about as much as I am. His brows are drawn down, and his jaw is set.

He eyes my outfit. "Smart choice."

I have my coat on, but he can tell I'm not in my uniform. I'm wearing dark leggings with a cropped sweater underneath. I figured wearing my school uniform with my Russian flag colors would probably make things even more awkward than they already will be.

"I'm not an idiot."

He rolls his eyes and walks back the way he came, clearly expecting me to follow. I want so badly to turn around and go back into the dorm, but Dmitri—or worse, Pavel—would probably drag me out.

So instead, I offer a crude gesture to Dante's back and hurry to catch up with him.

We're quiet until the path splits, and we take the direction that leads toward the dining hall. It's so cold out tonight, our breaths leave puffs of white in the air.

"What can I expect from tonight?" I ask, hating that my voice betrays my nerves.

"I already gave everyone in my crew the heads-up that you'd be sitting with us. Figured it would head off some of the awkwardness."

"Okay . . . should I just keep my mouth shut the whole meal?" That's what I plan to do.

He shrugs, hands pushed into his coat pockets. "Just be yourself." Then he abruptly stops and turns to face me. I stop, too. "Maybe a little less than yourself. Try to keep the cutting remarks and digs to a minimum."

"Don't be a bitch, you mean?" I arch an eyebrow.

"Basically." He turns and walks again.

Hurt strikes me like the lash of a whip. I don't know why. I'm the one who's worked so hard to cultivate this image everyone has of me.

I don't say anything as I walk behind him. Before long, we approach the dining hall. My stomach flips like a child rolling down a hill, and I place my hand on my coat, over my belly.

Dante's hand is on the door handle, and he turns to look at me. His face is etched in stone, but when he takes me in, his expression softens. "You'll be fine. Know this, if anyone really steps out of line, I'll deal with them. No one's going to touch you or anything, so don't worry about that."

I'm thankful for his reassurance. It eases me slightly. I nod and motion for him to open the door. Then I tilt up my chin and muster up some false confidence to walk in there as though I don't give a shit what anyone thinks.

Dante swings the door open, and I step inside. He follows me, coming to stand at my side, when I swear every single head in the place turns in our direction. The constant murmur of conversations that serves as background noise slowly dissipates until you can hear a pin drop.

I force myself to look around the room and meet the eyes of some of the people openly gaping, praying I don't crack under the weight of all their stares and their obvious disdain. I'm sure the entire school knows of our engagement by now, and we've been in the dining hall hundreds of times on our own, but never together. Never to make a statement like this.

Dante takes my hand before pulling me forward and forcing me to walk down the center of the large room, between the rows of tables on either side. The feeling of my palm in his grounds me, as much as I hate that, and some of my terror dissipates with each step.

"Let's grab our food first, then we'll head over to the table," he says, directing us toward the opening that leads into the room where all the food is.

I nod, too afraid that if I try to speak, my voice will come out warbled.

We split up, Dante heading to the area that serves Italian cuisine and me heading over to the Thai food. They only serve Thai food once a week, and it's my favorite, so I always get it when it's available. I end up getting some pad Thai and khao pad, along with some kaeng lueang in a bowl. The scents waft up to me as I turn to find Dante in the sea of students getting their food.

There's no way I'm walking over to the Accardi table on my own.

I spot Dante standing near the doorway and looking for me. When my gaze meets his, a feeling of relief washes over me.

Since when do I feel relieved to be in Dante's presence? Since I feel like we're a tag team.

I head toward him, and he looks at my tray. "Didn't take you for a Thai fan."

I tilt my head. "Why not?"

He lifts a shoulder. "Not sure, just didn't. You ready to do this?"

I give him a sharp nod.

"Let's go." He motions toward the dining hall.

I step forward, leading the way out of the serving area, tired of being a scared little mouse. I've been scared of worse than what a bunch of people I don't know might think of me. There's no reason I should care about this . . . besides the fact that I'll be surrounded by all of these people for the duration of my life if I don't get out of this marriage to Dante.

He makes his way beside me, and when we reach the Accardi table, he pulls out a chair for me. We're sitting right in the middle of the table. Of course we can't be on the end or anything.

I place my tray on the table and take a seat; Dante helps to push in my chair. Everyone stops talking and peers at where Dante sits next to me. After we have our coats off and hung on the back of our chairs, he looks around the table, meeting the eyes of everyone there.

"Is there a problem?" he asks.

Everyone sort of stares, then goes back to their earlier conversations.

I don't know most of the people here, so Dante does the introductions. Directly across from him is his brother, Dom, and across from me is Dante's cousin Bianca. On the other side of Dante is Santino, another cousin, then on down the line. Everyone is pleasant enough to put on an air of civility when we're introduced, and no one says anything outright shitty to me.

I recognize the girl at the end of the table staring daggers at me as the same girl Dante was dancing with at the party. When it's time for her introduction, Dante introduces her as Isabelle and doesn't linger before moving on to the next person.

She's the only one at the table I detect any outright hostility from, so I relax back into my seat. Maybe I'll be able to sit quietly, not say a word, and eat my dinner.

Dante talks to his brother and cousin about nothing in particular, and I pretend to find my meal endlessly fascinating, barely looking up from my dish until Dante's cousin Bianca engages me.

"I've seen you around. Where do you do most of your shopping? You have some really nice pieces," she says. She points at the Fendi crop sweater I'm wearing.

"Oh, thanks. Mostly I shop in New York when I'm home."

"Well, you have great style." She sounds sincere, not like this is something Dante has put her up to.

But then again, why would he ask Bianca to say something nice to me? He may have already talked to all these people and told them not to start anything, but that's likely so it doesn't devolve into an outright brawl between the Russians and the Italians right here in the dining hall, not for any regard for my feelings.

"Thanks." I shove a bite of my food into my mouth, unsure of what to say next.

"I'm surprised you're wearing Fendi though . . ." Her gaze goes to Dante, who's still talking with the guys, as though maybe she's said something she shouldn't.

I can't help my chuckle. "Why, because it's an Italian fashion house?"

She shrugs. "Well, yeah."

"Good fashion is good fashion."

She smiles. "Agreed. Maybe us Italians and Russians have more in common than we think." Bianca winks.

I take it for what it is—an olive branch. A chance to connect over something we can agree on. And so, the two of us chat for a bit about our various favorite fashion brands. Bianca mentions a few California-based designers I'm not familiar with but plan to check out now that she's talked them up so well.

The entire time, I feel Isabelle's eyes on me. I try to ignore it at first, but the longer it goes on, the more it pisses me off. She doesn't have to be nice to me, but I'm not going to let her think she can intimidate me.

When there's a break in our conversation, I turn my head in Isabelle's direction and meet her stare head-on.

"Do you have something you want to say to me, Isabelle?" I keep my cold mask of indifference in place as I hold her gaze.

"Just surprised you have the balls to sit here after what your people did to Aria Costa—sorry, Vitale." She rolls her eyes as if Aria's marriage to the head of the Vitale family is of little significance.

"You failed to mention what your people did to my brother." There's an underlying fury in my voice, and though the words are for her, the anger is mostly directed at myself.

How can I make conversation when these are the people, if only by extension, who played a role in murdering my brother? How did I allow myself to forget?

Everyone at the table quiets and looks between us, including

Dante. I would have thought he'd shut down this conversation, but he seems content to let it run its course.

"He had it coming after what he did."

My hands fist around my cutlery. "Is that really what you're upset about? Or are you upset I've taken your boy toy away?" I nod toward Dante at my side.

She smirks. "Oh, you haven't taken anything away, don't worry."

I open my mouth to put her in her place, but Dante slams a fist against the table, making everyone's trays jump. "That's enough, Isabelle. You will treat my fiancée with the respect she should be afforded, do you understand?"

I can't see the expression on his face because he's turned his head toward her, but it must be withering because she looks rightfully repentant.

"Yes," she murmurs.

"Now apologize to Polina," he says.

Outrage flashes across Isabelle's features, but she presses her lips together before she looks at me with a "sorry" before stabbing her fork back into her meal.

I meet her gaze with a satisfied smirk designed to get under her skin, if only because what she said still echoes in my head . . . "You haven't taken anything away."

Is Dante really still fucking around with her? After the way he acted toward Sasha at the café yesterday? Ire coats my skin the rest of the meal, and I don't bother looking up from my plate, not interested in conversing with anyone.

Finally, it's time to leave, and I bid everyone goodbye—except for Isabelle. I'm afraid if she even looks at me wrong, I might strangle her.

Dante and I slip on our coats, and he takes my hand again to lead me out of the building.

As we leave, we pass some of the Russian tables. I force myself to look at them, and they're looking at me with outright hostility as if I've betrayed them. We're not even part of the same Bratva, so I don't know why they care so much.

That's a lie. I do.

When we pass the Aminoff table, Dmitri gives us a small nod of approval that must rankle Dante because his hand tenses around mine. Pavel glares at us for some unknown offense, and Sasha's worried gaze meets mine.

I turn away from all of them and stare straight ahead. There's only room for one thing in my mind right now, and that's Dante and Isabelle. I don't want to examine why the thought consumes me.

CHAPTER FIFTEEN
DANTE

The moment we walk out the doors of the dining hall, Polina rips her hand from mine.

"I thought that went well," I say. I hear a harrumph from Polina and look at her. "You didn't?"

She glances around at some of the people lingering on the path on their way back to the dorms and doesn't say anything until we're clear of them all.

"Are you still fucking Isabelle?"

It was obvious Isabelle's comment pissed her off, but I assumed that it was just because of how it made Polina look in front of everyone. But the fact that she's bringing it up now, when it's just the two of us, makes me think it's more than that.

"Would you care?" I'm genuinely curious as to her answer.

She stops walking and whips in my direction. "Of course I'd care. This isn't some arranged marriage anymore where we'll show up at the altar and that's the beginning of us. We're being forced to parade around like we're a happy couple, and you messing around with her undermines me. It makes me look weak and like a fool."

I step closer to her. "You sure that's the only reason?"

"You sure the only reason you were pissed about Sasha was because it looked bad?"

My jaw clenches so hard I'm surprised my teeth don't turn to dust. I think back to the way he had his hand over hers and how she was looking at him . . . squeezing my eyes shut, I will away the image before I lose my shit.

"I'm not fucking Isabelle. Though she did show up at my room the night we returned, offering herself up. I sent her packing."

Outrage is clear on Polina's face, and she turns and stomps back in the direction of the dining hall. "That stupid bitch."

I snag her around the waist and pull her back against my front. "Easy, tiger. There's no point in going and starting a brawl. I made it clear to Isabelle that wouldn't be happening anymore. She knows the score. That's why she was so pissed tonight."

To my surprise Polina doesn't try to pull away from me, and the longer we stand pressed together, the more my dick gets some stupid ideas, so I drop my arms and step back.

"You good now?" I ask.

She turns and faces me, cheeks pink—though I don't know if that's from the cold or something else. "Yeah, it's just . . . the nerve. Who goes after someone they know is engaged? Have some respect for yourself."

I don't disagree with her, so I say nothing for a beat.

There was something flitting through my brain earlier that I ended up dismissing, but now I wonder if I shouldn't ask her.

Fuck it.

"Do you want to go see a movie with me this week?"

She blinks, almost as if she's confused. "A movie?"

Over the summer, the academy built a large movie theater on campus in an effort to curb the violence that happened last year. I guess it was decided we are too isolated from the real world and that young adults, especially ones like us, need more things to do on campus.

"Yeah, the theater on campus is open now, and I haven't checked it out yet. Thought it would be a good way to spend time together like our families want. And just think, because it's a movie, we won't even have to talk for most of the night."

Polina gives me a wry smile. "Wasn't tonight enough togetherness for one week?"

I sigh, then push a hand through my hair. "I know neither of us is exactly thrilled about our predicament, but we're in it. I've been thinking that maybe we should give it a real try to see if we can somehow get along and coexist. It would make both of our lives easier, happier."

I don't know about her, but I am so sick of the ups and downs that have gone along with this engagement. We may never have chosen each other, but we're stuck together, so we might as well make the best of it. Maybe it took me too fucking long to realize it, but it's worth a shot.

Polina looks at me skeptically. "What gives?"

"What do you mean?"

She crosses her arms. "All of a sudden you want to set all the shit between us aside and give this a real go? Forgive me for being suspicious."

Guess I should've expected this reaction.

"Listen, it's obvious that we're attracted to each other physically—" I raise my hand when she opens her mouth to argue. "Cut the bullshit. I'm just saying . . . maybe that's something we can build on. Maybe we can at least get to a place where we can tolerate each other if we put in some effort. Not to mention your brother and my dad are going to force us to anyway. At least this way, we're not doing it kicking and screaming."

What I don't tell her is that tonight was the first time I could see how it might be once we were married and she's considered a part of the family. I should have known that Bianca would be the one to try to befriend her first. That's just her way. She's always picking up strays.

No one else at the table did the same, but they held their tongues, which is more than I expected they would. All except Isabelle. Stupid girl.

And for her part, Polina tried. No, she and Bianca won't be making friendship bracelets in their dorm rooms anytime soon, but she wasn't her usual cold, emotionless self. She tried. When I didn't think she would. I figured she wouldn't say a word the entire meal. But when Bianca extended a hand to her, Polina didn't slap it away.

"Before I agree, I want to know that you're not going to be sleeping with anyone else. I've heard how it is with the Italians. You guys are always cheating on your wives, and it's considered acceptable. But I'm not Italian, Dante; I'm Russian. And Russian women don't deal with infidelity by turning a blind eye."

I can't help the grin forming on my face. "Have I told you what a turn-on it is when you're jealous?" I step toward her, but she holds out her arm.

"I'm not jealous. It's about respect. You can't be pissed at me because Sasha is helping me with homework, then expect me to look the other way when women are showing up at your door propositioning you."

"You are jealous. It's okay. You don't have to admit it," I add quickly.

Her lips press together as though she wants to say something but stops herself.

"I've already made it clear to Isabelle that we won't be fooling around anymore. You have no worries there. As for anyone else, that's fine. I won't mess around with anyone. But you need to do the same. I want you to stay away from Sasha." My voice is hard now.

"I've been friends with Sasha for years. I can't just all of a sudden ignore him."

"Can and will." I step forward, and this time she doesn't push me away.

"No, I need his help." Something flashes across her features. I can't be sure what exactly, but it's there and gone.

I'm not exactly known for my academics, otherwise, I'd insist on helping her.

"Fine." The word goes against everything in me, and I feel as if I'm going to burst with aggression. "But you only study with him in public."

She holds my gaze then nods. "Fine."

"Fine." I return her nod. "Then it's agreed. Neither of us will screw around with anyone else while we're trying to make this work."

"Agreed."

After another step closer, we're basically nose to nose. "Should we seal this deal with a kiss? Start things off right?"

Her gaze goes from my eyes to my mouth, and she licks her bottom lip.

My dick twitches, and I manage to bite back a groan. "What do you say, tesoro?"

We lean in slowly, so slowly, millimeter by millimeter, until our lips almost touch.

But Polina steps back, giving her head a shake. "I'm freezing. Let's get going." And without looking back to see if I'm following, she walks down the path.

I grin because it's only a matter of time. I know she wants me. She just doesn't want to want me. But, eventually, she'll give in, and it will be even sweeter when she does.

CHAPTER SIXTEEN
POLINA

The only reason I agreed to Dante's demands last night was because it should help lower his guard and make what I'm trying to achieve with Sasha easier. At least that's what I tell myself. And I'd believe it if my stomach hadn't flipped when he asked me to see a movie with him. If I hadn't secretly preened when he admitted to being attracted to me, at least physically.

All of that just made me more aware of why I need to push forward with this plan with Sasha. Already I'm weakening toward Dante's advances, and that can only be disastrous for me.

Once again, I'm meeting Sasha at the café so he can help me "study." He offered to come to my dorm room, but I couldn't risk it getting back to Dante. Not yet anyway. I need him to trust me more than he does now.

So when there's a knock at my dorm room door as I'm finishing getting ready, I hope it's not Sasha. It will be hard to find an excuse to leave without telling him it's because it's what Dante wants while still making him think I'm into him.

But it's worse than that when I open the door. It's Pavel.

"What do you want?" I don't bother opening the door farther because I don't want him to come inside.

He smirks in that way that makes me see red, the same expression that's always made me feel weak and helpless. He crosses his arms and leans against the door frame. "I have a message for you."

"Great, deliver it and go. I have somewhere to be."

His eyes narrow, and panic wells up in me. Sometimes I forget who I'm dealing with, how cruel of a man he is. "Dmitri wants to make sure you're aware that you'll have to ask Dante to the Sadie Hawkins dance."

My jaw sets. It's not as if I would ask Sasha, but I hate when my brothers order me around as though women don't have a say. I had that say until they promised me to Dante Accardi.

This is the first year the school is holding a Sadie Hawkins dance. I think it's a part of their effort to keep things more entertaining and give us an outlet on campus, much like the movie theater, and also some lame attempt to act as though this school isn't full of old-school, outdated ideas about women and their role in this world.

"I figured as much. Goes along with being paraded around as the golden couple, right?"

Pavel straightens off the door frame and lets his hands drop to his sides. "Don't fuck this up, Polina."

Sometimes it's hard to believe we're twins. Aren't twins supposed to have some sort of special bond and be closer than most siblings?

"I just said I'd ask him."

He steps toward me as though he's going to push his way into my room, and I freeze. But then we hear "Pavel!" from down the hall, and our heads swing in that direction.

I've never been so happy to see Irina.

"Hey, you busy? I was going to see if you wanted to swing by my room. Oksana is out for a while."

"I'll leave you guys to it." I close my door on them and go back into my room to grab my bag.

When I open the door again, they're mercifully gone.

* * *

SASHA AND I have been studying for an hour when I suggest we take a break.

"Just for a bit. My brain feels like mush." I smile.

He's sitting beside me again, but I've been careful not to look too cozy in case Dante decides to show up. I have to tread lightly if I don't want Dante to forbid me from seeing Sasha.

"Okay, let's take a break then." He studies me. "How are you, Polina? Really?"

I sigh. "Scared. Unsure. In a situation I don't want to be in." None of that is a lie, it's just not for the reasons he's going to infer.

"I wish there was something I could do." Sasha stares into my eyes, and I know he wants to touch me, lean in and embrace me, maybe kiss me, but I have to hold him at bay.

I look away like the sheepish woman I'm not. "There's nothing anyone can do. My fate has been decided for me."

He brings my chin around so that I'm looking at him again. "Have you tried talking to Dmitri about it? You two used to be so close. I imagine there isn't anything he wouldn't do for you."

I frown. "I've tried. He's changed since he's taken over. Now all that matters to him is what's best for Bratva."

Sasha's jaw tenses. "I hate this for you."

"Me too. If I wasn't being forced to marry Dante . . ." I look away again.

"What?"

I shake my head, slowly looking back at him. "I shouldn't say it. It could get us both in big trouble."

"Say it, Polina," he says with a pleading tone.

"If I weren't being forced to marry Dante . . ." I make a show of swallowing hard. "Maybe we could've been together."

His eyes go wide. "I thought you didn't feel that way about me."

"I was just scared of how much I feel for you . . . but now . . . now it doesn't matter. All that stuff I said at the party, I said to protect you. If Dante ever found out . . ." I shudder.

"Fuck." He pushes a hand through his hair and stares at me. "All those times I approached you . . . why didn't you ever say something?"

"I told you. I was scared, and I didn't have any idea my brother was going to marry me off."

Sasha looks broken by my words, and I have to push back the feeling churning in my stomach, otherwise I might be sick all over him. I've never felt so guilty.

"I'm sorry," I nearly whisper. "I shouldn't have said anything." I mean the words, just not how he thinks.

"No, I'm glad you said something. I just . . . I don't know what to do."

I shake my head with a sad smile. "There's nothing to do."

We sit in silence for a beat, and I consider pushing this conversation forward even more, but I think it's best to let Sasha stew on this for a while. Imagine the possibilities if I'd confessed sooner or if Dante weren't around and standing in the way.

We should get back to studying anyway.

"Forget I said anything." I pull the textbook closer to me and flip the page.

I'm in my room later that night, second-guessing my plan, feeling guilty as hell but knowing I need to do something before I find myself completely under Dante's spell, when I get a text from the man in question.

> DANTE: I reserved us seats at the theater for tomorrow night. Meet me in front at 6:45 pm.

The small smile I can't fight is indication enough that I need to see this plan through, no matter how guilty I feel. It's the only way to protect myself.

CHAPTER SEVENTEEN

DANTE

The nine o'clock showing was already sold out, so I had to book us for the earlier showing of a new romantic comedy. I'd rather have seen the action movie playing in the other theater, but I figured Polina would probably appreciate this one more. I'm purposely blocking out why I'm doing what she would want.

She arrives on time. I thought she might be late or ditch me altogether just to be difficult. She's wearing those leggings that hug her curves perfectly with some boots with the socks showing over top of them, and when she removes her coat inside the building, I see that she's wearing an oversized sweater that exposes one shoulder. Still designer, though, of course.

Seeing her bare shoulder is surprisingly hot. The only downside of her sweater is that it covers her ass, and Polina's ass in leggings is something amazing. Although I do prefer to be the only one enjoying the view.

"Do you want to get some snacks before we go to our seats?" I ask her.

"Sure."

There aren't many people around—probably because it's a Friday night, and it's a seven o'clock showing—so it doesn't take us long to get to the front of the line. A lot of people will still be in the dining hall or just shooting the shit about what they're going to do tonight.

"What'll it be?" I motion to the display of candy.

"Popcorn and some licorice."

I nod and order what we both want, plus some water for each of us. Popcorn always makes you thirsty, and I don't want her using her need for water as an excuse to disappear for a half hour to the concession stand.

"Thanks," she says. "I assume we're seeing the action movie?"

I shake my head, taking our stuff from the counter and turning to walk over to the napkins. "You assume wrong."

"Really? The romantic comedy?" She stops and stares at me for a beat.

I nod.

"That was nice of you."

I shrug, grabbing some napkins from the dispenser. "Take it this once. I'm not always nice."

She shakes her head and laughs, finally understanding my humor a little. "Well, thank you."

"Let's go. I'm sure you'll love the torture of me having to watch this one." I wink, then turn in the direction of our theater.

A small chuckle escapes her as she walks beside me, and I pretend I'm not as pleased as I am that I made her laugh twice.

Once we're in the dim theater, I lead her to our seats.

I booked us the best seats you can get. Our chairs recline, and the armrest between the two seats comes up to make it one big loveseat. We're provided with some small pillows and blankets, and there are tables on the outside of each seat. Each twosome is surrounded by a privacy wall of sorts that curves around so it almost feels as though you're alone in the theater.

"This looks cozy." Polina stares at the seats.

"Figured you'd want the private ones so everyone wasn't gawking at us. I noticed how uncomfortable that makes you."

"You did?" She looks at me, and yet again, her beautiful features line with surprise.

"Don't worry, you put up a good front. I'm sure no one else knows. I've just observed you enough now that I can read you a little better." I shrug and motion to the seats. "So I booked these."

"I'm starting to feel indebted to you," she says, but with a smile. She should smile all the time. It makes her undeniably stunning.

I sit in my seat and toss a piece of popcorn into my mouth before I press the button to raise the footrest. "I can be an asshole, Polina, but I'm not always an asshole."

She takes a seat to my left. "Yeah, I'm starting to see that."

"Jesus." I shake my head.

"What?" She hangs her jacket on the hook on the inside of the wall that curves around us.

"Only you could make it sound like me not being an asshole is a bad thing." I chuckle.

"You're just . . . not exactly what I expected, that's all." She places her water in the cupholder to her right, situating herself in her seat.

"Yeah, well, neither are you." I toss another couple pieces of popcorn in my mouth.

"What did you expect?" She looks at me expectantly.

"Honestly?"

She nods.

"Figured you'd be a raging bitch pretty much all the time. Either that or have no emotion at all."

Polina chuckles, but it doesn't reach her eyes. "I can understand that."

She doesn't say anything more, and I don't pry further.

The preshow stuff comes on, and Polina pulls the blanket over her, shivering.

"Cold?" I ask.

She nods. "Why do they always make it like a walk-in freezer in these theaters?"

I laugh. "No idea, but you're right. It's always freezing."

"I have to ask you something, and please know it's okay to say no. I don't care."

My forehead wrinkles. What on earth could she be asking me? "Okay."

"Would you go to the Sadie Hawkins dance with me next weekend?" She bites that plump bottom lip of hers, and I don't know if she's hoping I'll say yes or no.

I have no doubt Dmitri instructed her to ask me, so I try not to read her invitation as anything but fulfilling our roles.

"Yeah, I'm your fiancé after all. Who else would you go with?" I inject a little more steel into my voice than intended.

"Right. Okay then, it's a date." She nods as though she's glad that's done and out of the way.

"Date number two." I put two fingers in the air.

"Is this date number one?" she asks.

"Guess we'll see how the night goes, won't we?" I wink.

The previews end, and the lights dim further. I can't help but wonder if she's thinking the same thing as me—were we just flirting with each other?

* * *

I LEAN OVER the armrest and whisper in Polina's ear, "You have to admit that this is terrible."

She turns her head to look at me with her mouth hanging open. "It's not that bad. Just because it doesn't have exploding cars and machine guns."

Just then, the guy on screen delivers the cheesiest line ever, and I roll my eyes at her. "See what I mean?"

She shakes her head. "You are such a guy. It's romantic."

About twenty minutes later comes a heavy make-out scene, and though the dialogue in this movie isn't worth shit, they've done a good job with this particular scene. It's hot as fuck, even if there is no actual fucking in it, and I have to shift in my seat to make room for the half chub I've got going on.

Polina's breath hitches, a clear indication that this scene is affecting her, too. As if that weren't confirmation enough, I watch from the corner of my eye as she squeezes her legs together. I'm not sure how much longer I'll be able to keep my hands off of her.

CHAPTER EIGHTEEN
POLINA

I've been uncomfortable ever since the first make-out scene in this movie. Not because I'm sitting so close to Dante. No, he's been surprisingly good company tonight, considering what I'd like to watch and picking this movie. I would never admit that the movie *is* pretty cheesy and lame. And how he grabbed me water without asking because he figured I'd be thirsty after eating popcorn, which I was.

He could've used the opportunity when I asked him to the dance to make me feel stupid, but he didn't. In fact, it really kind of seemed like maybe he is looking forward to going with me.

All that makes it difficult to stem the ache between my legs. Dante looks so good tonight. He's wearing jeans that are worn in all the right places and fit him perfectly and a gray Henley that brings out the gray undertone of his light blue eyes. I haven't masturbated lately because every time I do, images of Dante are all I see.

Maybe it's just me, but the entire time I've been sitting during this movie, I've been hyper aware of how close he is to me, almost as though I can feel the difference when he shifts in his seat or if he moves an inch or two. The scent of his cologne is masculine and a little woodsy, a little musky, but so wholly him that even when I close my eyes, I feel as if I'm surrounded by him.

Then the sex scene comes on. Not totally uncommon for a romance movie, but usually it fades to black. Not this one. This one has full frontal nudity for the woman, and you even see some partial ass clenching when the male lead pushes into her.

I shift in my seat, needing to expel some of the energy and tension that's building up inside me. Without saying anything, Dante lifts the armrest between us and shifts closer to me.

I turn to look at him. "What are you doing?"

He leans in and whispers in my ear, "What you want but won't ask for."

At first, I frown, not knowing what he means. But when he skims his hand over my breast, my treacherous body arches into his touch. I bite back a moan when his thumb flits back and forth over my puckered nipple.

It's not until his hand continues down under the blanket on my lap, and his fingertips breach the elastic of my leggings, that I come to my senses. I reach under the blanket and wrap my hand around his wrist.

"Stop. We shouldn't do this." For more reasons than I can verbalize.

Because he's still my enemy even if he is my fiancé. Because I'm plotting to kill him. Because if I let him do this, I'm admitting I want it. I don't have drunkenness as an excuse to fall back on. And the biggest one—because I know that if he does this, once will never be enough. I'll only crave him more than I do now.

He kisses the spot on my jaw just under my ear. "Shh. I know what you need."

I fight to suppress the shiver that courses through my entire body, but I don't fool him. His low chuckle sounds in my ear as he pushes his hand under the seam of the pink silk fabric, too.

That first touch of his finger coasting over my clit pulls a sharp moan from me.

"Shh. Don't want everyone to know what we're doing, do we?" he says into my ear.

He applies more pressure and circles the nub, and my back arches.

"You're already so wet, tesoro. Were you imagining me with my hands down your pants, finger-fucking you where anyone could get up out of their seat and walk past us? Do you think they'd know what I'm doing to you under this blanket just by the look on your face?"

His words have my eyes closing and my head pushing back into the headrest.

When he pushes one, then two fingers into me, I bite my bottom lip to prevent myself from making a sound that would give us away. He moves his fingers inside me, and I suck in a sharp breath.

God, it feels so good. My head thrashes side to side on the headrest as I attempt to keep my orgasm at bay. I can't come already because then it will be over, and I want Dante to keep this up all night.

He picks up the pace, fucking me with his fingers so hard that I rise up on the seat every time he pushes them in. When he pulls them from me completely, I almost cry out in protest.

But he moves to my clit again, massaging me there until I can't help but pant. For the first time since he started this, I turn my head and look at him. Our eyes catch and hold. His with the hot burn of intensity, mine I think somewhat pleading. For more, for climax, for this to never end. I don't know.

"That's it. Good girl. You're doing so well keeping quiet."

I nod frantically. I'd probably agree with almost anything right now if he'd let me finish.

"Do you know fucking beautiful you look when you're about to come?" He nips on my bottom lip.

I soak in his praise, greedy and wanting more.

He does something with his fingers, I'm not even sure what, but it has my orgasm barreling down on me like a rogue wave, then it hits me. I climax and fall apart, squeezing my eyes shut, back bowing and shaking as pleasure rolls through me, thick and heady.

"Good girl."

Those two words have my orgasm drawing out even longer. Eventually, my eyes drift open slowly as Dante pulls his hands out from under my leggings and under my blanket.

"I refuse to taste you off my fingers. The first time I taste you will be with my mouth as you're splayed out in front of me." He brings the two fingers he had inside me up to my mouth and feeds them to me, pushing them past my lips.

The sweet, tangy taste hits my tongue, and his nostrils flare. I suck on his fingers, though he doesn't tell me to, and when I do, a low groan echoes out of him, lust-consumed eyes watching me with fascination.

He slowly removes his fingers from my mouth and uses that hand to adjust himself in his pants. "Fuck, I'm going to be running that through my head for a solid week." He grins at me.

That's when the mortification finally sets in. What I let him do to me. What I did.

"I have to go to the bathroom." I bolt up out of my seat and rush out of the theater.

When I reach the bathroom, I stare at myself in the mirror, hands planted in front of me on the counter. *Why did I let Dante touch me like that?*

I squeeze my eyes shut, ashamed. Ashamed because I liked it. Ashamed because now I'm craving more of him. What is wrong with me? I'm trying to extract myself from this situation, not dive further into it. My head is a whirlwind of confusion.

My eyes burn, and my throat constricts. I can't remember the last time I cried. I couldn't have been more than ten or eleven before I figured out the best way to protect myself was to feel numb. But if I could cry, I think I would right now.

Once I've composed myself, I decide the best thing is to act like nothing happened. Not very mature, no, but I can't stand the idea of Dante lording this over me or poking at me about this.

Walking out of the restroom, I come to an abrupt stop when I find Dante standing there.

"Everything okay?" He seems genuinely concerned.

"All that popcorn and licorice upset my stomach." I place my hand over my belly. "I think I should probably get going."

He remains leaning against the wall, his eyes narrowed as if I'm a math problem he can't figure out. I'm lying, and he knows it. The question is whether he'll call me out.

Dante pushes off the wall and nods. "Okay, I'll walk you back."

I shake my head and walk in the direction of the theater so I can grab my jacket. "Not necessary. You stay and finish the movie."

He catches up to me. "We both know I'm not going to allow you to walk back by yourself, Polina."

I want to close my eyes and savor the gentle way he says my name, but I don't. I keep walking until we're in the theater, grabbing our jackets, then I hurry past him back out of the theater.

"Where's the fire?" he asks, catching up with me.

"No fire, I'm just not feeling well, like I said."

"Mmmhmm."

He makes it to the door to the outside first and holds it open for me. There are more people around now, making their way to the building, and I put on my usual unaffected air.

We walk in silence back to Moskva House, the space between us no longer feeling threaded with sexual tension but with unhinged anger. Dante wants to ask questions, demand answers from me, but he doesn't.

We reach the front of Moskva House, and I turn to face him. "Thanks for the movie."

Before he can say anything, I spin on my heels and push through the entrance of my dorm, needing some separation from him in order to get my head on straight.

I need to remember the end game—and it's not Dante Accardi.

CHAPTER NINETEEN

DANTE

Polina ate dinner at my table a couple of times this week, but that's been the extent of our interaction since the movie. She didn't say much, except to Bianca, who again engaged her in conversation. A couple of the guys said something to Polina near the end of the second night this week, but she all but ignored me.

I should be pissed. Probably would be if I didn't think that a little distance between us might be a good thing. Although I was the one who suggested we try getting along to see what might be between us, I meant it more in the way of finding out if we can stand each other and be cordial since we have the rest of our lives together.

But since the movie, she's had this hold on me. I can't stop thinking about her. About how she looked when she came. How she might taste on my tongue or feel around my cock. And not just that. I find myself curious about her. What kind of things make her happy, sad, pissed off. How can I get her to drop her walls, so I can really get to know her?

Things I have no business thinking about.

Or do I?

We're getting married after all. Maybe this change of heart where Polina is concerned is a good thing. But can I trust her? Can I ever really trust her, or will she always have the Russians' best interests at heart and not mine, not *ours*? That's my hang-up. I've been told since

I could talk not to trust anyone—not even people in our own family at times—and suddenly I have a fucking Russian as a fiancée, and I'm expected to share my life, my vulnerabilities, with her.

But tonight is the night of the Sadie Hawkins dance, so I should have lots of time to further my assessment of my fiancée.

It was obvious that my finger-fucking her at the movie shook her, even as much as she'd enjoyed it. And though it's in my nature to push, something in my gut told me that the better call was to let her deal with it on her own—at least this time. If she thinks she's going to bail immediately after every time we mess around, she'll soon learn how wrong she is.

Polina told me to meet her outside the gymnasium where the dance is to be held, probably in an effort to shorten our time together tonight. Standing at the door, I've said hello to a few people I know who have already headed inside. Marcelo and Mirabella stroll up, hand in hand.

"Fiancée keeping you waiting?" Marcelo says with a smirk.

I hate this prick.

"Not as long as you've kept Mira waiting to say 'I do.'" I wink at her just to piss him off.

Marcelo steps toward me, but Mira places a hand on his chest. "Let's just go inside."

He glares at me, and I return the look.

Then Mira diverts her attention to me. "Your mouth is going to get you in serious trouble one day."

They walk toward the doors, and I call after them, "You wouldn't believe what else my mouth is capable of, Mira. Too bad you never let me show you."

Marcelo tries to turn around, but Mira tugs him toward the door, and he follows. She glares over her shoulder at me, and I laugh.

"Friends of yours?"

I whip my head around to find Polina standing on my other side.

I don't know if there is such a thing as Russian royalty, but if there is, she would look the part.

She's dressed in a one-shoulder silver dress that hugs every one of her curves. One arm is bare and the other has a long sleeve. When she moves, the dress sparkles in whites and pale blues, the fabric changing hues. She's got on fuck-me strappy silver heels that look amazing, but her feet must have frozen on the walk over. Her hair is pulled back in a low bun, tight on the sides, showcasing her slender neck. If she wore a crown, she'd look like a Nordic princess.

"Wow." She fidgets as my gaze travels up and down her body, taking her all in. "You look phenomenal."

Her cheeks turn pink, and she looks down at herself, smoothing her dress over her belly. "Thanks."

"Hey." I take her hand. "Own it. You're about to ignite the war because every Russian bastard in here tonight is going to be jealous that an Italian has you on his arm."

She laughs, and I can't help but smile at her. Polina's laugh transforms her face. Gone is the cold, emotionless woman so many know, revealing what I think is the real Polina, if she would let the rest of the mask fall. The question I have is why she felt the need to develop such a thick exterior in the first place. I don't know, but I plan to find out.

"Shall we go in so I can make every man in there jealous of me? Probably some girls, too." I wink at her and offer her my arm.

She loops her arm through mine, and we walk into the gymnasium. The athletic space has been transformed into what could pass for a wedding. There are tables set along the far wall with ice sculpture centerpieces where people can hang out. Already I can see the dividing lines between all the factions. Giant balloon clusters dot different areas along the walls, and the lights are dim with white lights reminiscent of a disco ball moving over everything. In the corner is a DJ booth, and at the moment, a current hip-hop hit blasts from the speakers.

"You like hip-hop?" Polina leans in and asks, I assume because my head is bobbing to the music.

"Yeah, it's my preference. You?"

She shrugs. "I'm not that into music, but I mostly listen to pop."

"That's okay, I can help you improve your musical taste." I touch her arm that's looped around my own. "Do you want to grab a drink or something to eat?" I nod toward the refreshments tables.

"I'm okay for now."

"All right. Let's go find everyone."

I watch as her chest rises with a deep inhale. I'm not sure why she's nervous to hang around with my crew now that she's had several meals with us.

"Do you prefer to hang around with the people on your side?" I ask.

She shakes her head. "No, that's okay."

I frown, surprised she didn't take me up on my offer. "Let's do this then."

After the first hour passes, Polina becomes more comfortable, talking a little more with Bianca. From what I can overhear, they're discussing some up-and-coming designer in New York. When Polina's not chatting with Bianca, she's content to stand there quietly.

When the first slow song plays, I take her hand. "Let's go dance."

Polina looks panicked at first and glances around the entirety of the gym, but I gently tug on her arm, and she reluctantly comes along with me. She's going to have to get used to people looking at us and judging us at some point.

I wrap my arms around her waist and let them hang on her lower back. She stiffens before she brings her hands up to my shoulders and relaxes into my hold. We sway back and forth. I try not to concentrate on how the movements make her body rub against mine, otherwise my hard-on will push into her belly in short order.

"How do you see your life after we're married?" I ask her, trying to divert my attention to something else.

She looks up at me. "What do you mean?"

"Do you want to have children right away? Do you want a big family? Do you see yourself working outside the home?"

"Are those all a possibility?"

"Depends, I guess. I mean, certain precautions would have to be in place, but we have our hands in enough different industries that I'm sure I could find you a place somewhere you'd be safe."

Her eyebrows rise. "I thought all you Italians wanted your women barefoot and pregnant in the kitchen all the time."

"Some do, though I think that's changing these days. I've just always wanted a happy wife. I knew there was little chance that I'd ever get to pick my own bride, but I don't want to spend my life arguing and fighting with someone. Happy wife, happy life, right?"

"That's what they say . . ."

"So what would make you happy?"

Her lips twist to the side. "I'm not sure, honestly. I've never given it too much thought because it didn't seem like something I would have to worry about."

"You seem to really like fashion. Would you want to do something with that?"

An emotion I can't read crosses her face, but it's gone in a flash. "Maybe. We'll see."

"Hey." I stop us from moving and force her to look at me, turning her face my way with my thumb and forefinger. "I thought we were going to give this a go? See if we can find some common ground. Ever since the movie—"

Her eyes narrow. "I don't want to talk about that."

"We need to. Seems like it freaked you out how much you loved getting off on my fingers."

Polina pushes against my chest. "Why do you have to be so crude?"

I grab her wrists. "Stop pretending like you don't love it," I say through clenched teeth.

She rips her hands from my grasp. "I don't. And I need a break from you. I'm going to the restroom, then I'm getting something to drink. Don't come looking for me. I'll be back."

I grab her arm one more time, pulling her in close to me. "You can't keep running every time I tell you the truth and you don't like it. And I'm your fucking fiancé. I'm not sure how it is in your world, but in mine, you respect me."

Her face turns bright red before she spins on her heel and stomps off toward the door.

I shake my head as she gets farther away from me.

Turns out I'm done with not pushing her. Polina needs a good shove into reality.

CHAPTER TWENTY
POLINA

God, why does Dante always have to push so hard? Can't he just do what most people do and pretend nothing is going on, that everything is fine?

I hated those words coming out of his mouth because they were the truth. I do like it when he's blunt and says it like it is. Even if I don't like the truth of his words. Dante doesn't leave confusion about his motivations or what he's thinking. He just lays it all out on the table.

He surprised me when he said I could do something outside of the home after we're married. When I was told he'd be my husband, I pictured my days alone in some big house with little contact with the outside world. But the fact that he's not going to restrict me to that kind of life, that I could have something of my own, build something I'm proud of . . . well, I've never allowed myself to dream about the possibilities. Maybe now I can.

It's just hard to trust someone who is supposed to be my enemy, even if he is to be my husband. There have been people in my life I should have been able to trust, and I did without reservation—until they proved I shouldn't have.

I leave the bathroom with a feeling of optimism. Maybe I can have a life I enjoy with Dante. I'll just have to make sure I don't get emotionally attached. Is that possible if I find myself drawn to him physically?

I walk down the hallway toward the gym and find Sasha there, talking to one of his friends. Seeing him is like a record scratch on my brain. What about my plan? Do I toss it aside with the hope that Dante is a man of his word? Or do I continue on the course I've charted?

Sasha says something to his friend, then he heads my way while his friend goes back into the gym.

"Hey," I say, nervous and looking over his shoulder in case Dante makes an appearance.

"You look beautiful tonight."

I smile at him. It's hard not to compare how Dante's similar words made me feel to Sasha's. When Dante said every man would be jealous, my heart picked up its pace. But Sasha's words aren't even a blip on my radar.

"Are you having fun?" I ask him.

"I'd be having more fun if I were here with you." He steps forward and takes my hand.

I instantly step back and pull it from his grasp. "Sasha, we can't. Dante might see," I whisper, as if saying his name any louder will summon him.

"I don't give a fuck. I've watched you with him all night, watched his arms around you, watched as he parades you around like you're his."

"I am his," I say in a soft voice.

His nostrils flare, and his hands fist at his sides. "What if you weren't? What if you were mine?"

My heart gallops in my chest. This is what I wanted, right? This is where my trail of breadcrumbs was supposed to lead him. So why do I feel panic and not satisfaction?

"But I am. Dmitri has promised me to him."

He takes another step closer, entirely too close for this to be a casual, friendly conversation. He peers down at me, face serious. "What if Dante was no longer an issue?"

My entire body stills. "What do you mean?"

"What if he was out of the picture? What if something happened to him? Then we could be together, right?"

I suck in a breath. I wanted this. This is what I was working toward. Then why don't I feel like celebrating? Now all I have to do is nudge Sasha in the right direction without actually telling him to kill Dante. Plausible deniability, that's all I need.

I open my mouth to respond . . .

"What the fuck's going on?"

Dante's voice from behind Sasha sends a cold sweat over my body. I step back from Sasha, and Dante comes into view. He stands to the side, looking between Sasha and myself.

"I said, what the fuck is going on?"

I step closer to Dante, attempting to de-escalate the situation. "Nothing, I just ran into Sasha on the way back from the bathroom. We were figuring out the best time to get together so he could help me with my course. Right, Sasha?"

I look at him with a pleading expression on my face. It takes a minute, but eventually, he gives a brisk nod.

Dante's not satisfied though. "You sure about that?" He steps closer to Sasha. "Seems to me like maybe you're making a play for my fiancée. That couldn't be it, though, right? You're not that stupid."

Sasha doesn't back down, stepping closer toward Dante.

Shit. I squeeze between the two of them, facing Dante.

"Stop this. You're being stupid and getting pissed off over nothing." When Dante doesn't even glance down at me, still staring at Sasha behind me, I place my hands on his face. "Dante, don't do this. It'll escalate, and this entire dance will turn into a brawl. You're upset over nothing."

Still, he doesn't take his angry gaze off Sasha.

"You're my fiancé. There's nothing going on between Sasha and me. I'll prove it."

And I do the only thing I can think of to get Dante's attention off Sasha while at the same time showing Dante I have no qualms about proving my loyalty in front of Sasha. I go up on my tiptoes and pull Dante's face down so I can reach his lips, and I kiss him. At first, Dante doesn't react, his eyes still staring at Sasha with blazing intensity. He possessively darts his tongue into my mouth while keeping his gaze on Sasha. He wants to make sure Sasha sees his claim on me. It shouldn't be so hot, but an ache builds between my legs at Dante's declaration that I am his.

I open my mouth, and when our tongues meet, we sink into the kiss, eyes closing. He wraps one arm around me so his hand is splayed over my ass, and the other comes to the side of my face. Our kiss starts out slowly but gains intensity. I find myself arching into his chest, desperate to feel him everywhere.

When he pulls away, we're both breathing hard, staring at each other.

"You're coming with me." Dante lifts me up over his shoulder without warning, and I yelp.

"What the hell?" I raise my head and find us alone in the hallway. I don't know where Sasha went. If I'm honest, I forgot about him. Dante stalks down the hall, his hand on my ass in an effort to keep it from showing with the short dress I have on.

"Put me down!" I shout and punch what I now know is a very firm ass, but he doesn't relent.

"You'll have to get your coat later. I have no intention of putting you down so you can run. We'll take the long route through the school."

"Where are you taking me?"

"To my room."

The predatory and possessive way he says those words probably shouldn't turn me on, but it does. Still, I struggle to get out of his grip, but I quickly tire out.

He walks in silence, me bobbing on his shoulder. There's a short distance where we'll have to walk outside from the building to the Roma House, and when we reach it, he runs, using both hands to keep me steady. I have no idea how he's able to carry me this distance. He's stronger than I realized.

Then we're through a set of doors, and I assume we're inside Roma House. I don't dare try to raise my head, too mortified to do so. What must I look like to anyone who sees us? Like the spoils of war that have been plundered and him like a caveman taking what he deems to be his.

Then we're in the quiet small space of an elevator by ourselves.

"I don't want you seeing him again. You'll find someone else to help you study, got it?" When I don't answer right away, he smacks my ass. "Say yes."

He hit me hard enough that it stung, even through my dress, but left in its wake is a warm burn and an itch for him to do it again.

"You can't tell me what to do," I snipe.

He must have pushed the button to stop the elevator because our ascent suddenly stops.

"I won't make a habit of it, but if it means keeping you away from a man who is obviously waiting for an opportunity to slip his dick into your wet pussy, then I'll do just that. Especially when I haven't even had the privilege myself. But we're going to remedy that tonight, aren't we, tesoro?"

"What? No, we're not." I jerk in his hold until one hand slowly caresses my calf and makes its way up my leg. A shuddering breath leaves me.

I don't fight as his hand coasts up under my dress and onto the globe of my ass. He squeezes, and I bite back a moan.

"Are you trying to tell me that you're not already wet?" His gravelly voice feels as if it has a direct line to my core. He slides his hand between my legs, under the thin line of my silk underwear. "Mmm,

I'm gonna feast on this pussy before I make you come around my cock. Are you going to be a good girl and let me do that, Polina?"

Jesus, when he calls me a good girl, I swear I might do anything he wants. Those two little words strip me of all sensibility.

"Yes," I whisper, just loud enough for him to hear.

He removes his hand from between my legs and must press the elevator button, because it moves again.

My breath is ragged when Dante steps off the elevator and walks down the hall. After a brief pause in front of his door, he steps in, and I watch him close it with his foot. Seconds later, he's bending at the waist and setting my feet on the floor.

He holds me as I stumble to the side, a little woozy now that the blood is rushing away from my head. "Easy."

It takes me a moment to get my bearings, but when I do, I look up at him and nod. "Yeah, I'm good now."

An almost feral look transforms his face, and one corner of his mouth rises. "Good."

He lifts me by the waist and tosses me on my back onto his large bed. "I'm going to show you how good girls get rewarded, Polina. And remember that if I ever see you with that fucking goon again, you won't be my good girl anymore, and you don't want that, do you?"

I find myself shaking my head without even making a conscious decision to do so.

"Perfect." His eyes remain on me as he strips off his suit jacket.

I swallow hard, equal parts afraid of and looking forward to him making good on his promises.

CHAPTER TWENTY-ONE
DANTE

I toss my suit jacket on the chair to the side of the night table and peel off my tie before doing the same. Polina lies waiting for me while I slowly undo the buttons of my dress shirt, her chest heaving as she intently watches me. When I push my shirt open, and she gets a look at my bare chest, she bites her bottom lip.

I'm going to rock her fucking world, and when she's walking around tomorrow, she's going to remember who made her come so many times she couldn't see straight because she'll feel me between her thighs with every step. She won't even be able to think of that Sasha clown without comparing him to me and knowing my dick is bigger, and my mouth is better.

Tossing my shirt aside, I drop to my knees on the floor beside the bed then grab her ass and pull her to the edge. Her dress rides up to her hips, revealing her lacy white panties. My hands land on her inner thighs, prying them apart, forcing them to spread for me. She inhales a sharp breath, and I look up at her, licking my lips after seeing the wet white fabric between her thighs.

I debate whether to get her completely naked now or not, but I opt to let her keep her dress and her fuck-me shoes. I want to defile my ice princess when she looks so pretty and perfect.

I kiss the inside of her knee on one leg, then the other, slowly working my way closer to her center. My cock is hard and throbbing, pushing against the zipper of my suit pants, but I ignore it for now. It'll get its turn between her legs. Right now, my tongue is going to enjoy her.

I give her inner thigh a little nibble when I reach as far as I can without touching her pussy. She attempts to close her thighs, but I force her to keep spread wide with my palms. I place my mouth at the apex of her thighs and tongue the scrap of fabric between her legs. She moans and arches her back off the bed.

I tease her, running my nose along the wetness of the silk, inhaling her sweet scent until I'm ready to lose control from the unbearable need to taste her. Hooking my finger around her panties, I slowly pull the scrap of fabric down her legs, past the high heels she still wears, and toss them behind me. They'll be my souvenir.

Her glistening pink pussy greets me, ready for the taking. I make sure to hold her crystal-blue gaze as I lick from her entrance up to her clit. Polina's eyes drift closed, as do mine at the exquisite taste of her. Sweet and citrusy with an aftertaste of musk. My Russian princess is fucking perfect.

I want to take my time with her, teasing her with my tongue, spending time sucking her clit, but I lose all control and devour her like a man starved. Polina's hand pushes into the hair at the top of my head, pulling on the strands when I suck on her clit before returning to flicking it with my tongue. Her response drives me further, and I fuck her entrance with my tongue, driving it in as though it were my cock.

Her back arches off the bed, and she moans loudly, tugging harder on my hair when I return to her clit. She's getting closer. I tease her with my finger, running small circles around her entrance before I plunge it inside her. She cries out, and I draw back on the pressure I'm applying to her clit with my tongue. I want her desperate and begging for it. Then I add a second finger.

Her eyes spring open, peering down the beautiful length of her body at me. "Dante, please."

I grin against her core. She's so perfect when she's begging me for her orgasm. It's clear to me she has a little praise kink, whether she realizes it or not, so I decide to use it to help drive her over the edge.

Moving back, I stare at her spread legs, offering her up to me. "Look at you, tesoro. Such a pretty pussy, just begging me to make it come. Is that what you want? Do you want me to make you come?"

"Yes . . ." she moans, rocking her hips, but my hands hold them firmly in place.

"I want you to come all over my face. Can you be a good girl and do that?"

She nods somewhat desperately, and I grin, lowering my mouth back to her clit. I suck and use my tongue the way I've figured out she likes best, then I thrust two fingers into her roughly.

She's not a virgin, that much I can tell, but I don't want details. I'm likely to take names and track down each and every one of them for knowing what it feels like to thrust between these thighs.

I finger-fuck her, not holding back, and suck on her clit. Within seconds, she's crying out, riding my face as her orgasm takes over. I follow her body's lead as she slowly comes down from her high, then I place a chaste kiss on her pussy before straightening.

She opens her eyes and takes me in for a minute, then attempts to pull down her dress and close her legs.

"Oh no, princess. We're just getting started."

CHAPTER TWENTY-TWO
POLINA

Dante keeps my thighs spread, looking at me like a predatory wolf.

A shiver works its way through my body. I'm surprised I didn't pass out after that orgasm. I don't have a wealth of experience to draw from, but no guy has ever made me come like that. I've never even made myself come that hard.

Granted, I had no shame while his face was between my legs, but after, when he was studying me with such intensity, it felt like too much, and I wanted to hide. I'm not used to feeling vulnerable or sharing any kind of intimacy with anyone, but Dante seems like an open book.

"Get undressed." It's clear from his tone that it's not a request.

Before I can even think about it, I'm sitting up on the bed, shifting to my knees and undoing the zipper on the side of my dress.

"What about you?" I ask when I have the zipper all the way down.

"I'll get there. I want to admire you first." He squeezes his hard-on jutting against the fabric of his pants.

I swallow hard when I see the size of it. The fabric of my dress sags, and I gently pull my arm from the one sleeve, exposing my bare breasts to Dante. He steps forward and leans in, bringing his mouth to my right nipple and tugging on it with his teeth, then easing the pain with his tongue. My eyes flutter closed as he moves to my other breast while shimmying the fabric of my dress down past my hips.

When he pulls away, I lie back on the bed, and he drags the fabric down my legs. "Shoes stay."

My core clenches, and I watch in fascination as he unbuckles his belt, undoes the button on his pants, and lowers the zipper. He toes out of his shoes, removes his socks, then pushes both his pants and boxer briefs down his legs until gravity takes hold, and they pool around his feet.

His proud cock arches toward his belly button, rigid and firm and big. Holy shit, he's big.

I can't help but lick my lips as his hand moves to its base, and he strokes up and down his impressive length.

He comes closer, his thumb brushing along my bottom lip. I want to open, suck it into my mouth, twirl around it with my tongue. "I'll put those lips to good use soon, but for now, I want your cunt to squeeze me dry."

His crude words should make me want to shove my dress back on and storm out, but they have the opposite effect. Based on his grin, he knows it.

"Are you on the pill?" he asks.

I nod. With my dad gone, it wasn't as hard for me to procure birth control. It wasn't really something my brothers ever wanted to talk about, and when I told them I needed it because I had bad periods—a lie—they didn't argue.

"You have to use a condom, though." He frowns, so I explain further. "You've been with a lot of girls. I don't want to take any chances."

He looks as though maybe he wants to argue, but he doesn't. "When I'm home for the break between semesters, I'll get checked out so you know there's nothing to worry about."

"Okay." I've never had a guy inside me without a condom, and I'm curious how it might feel.

He walks over to his nightstand and pulls out a box of condoms.

It's already open, and it's a monumental effort not to think about how many of them might be gone and who he used them with. Dante rips open the package with his teeth and rolls the condom onto his considerable length, then stalks toward the bed.

My breath comes in fast, short spurts as he crawls onto the bed and hovers over me.

"Who owns this pussy, tesoro?" He lightly trails his nose along my jawline, propping himself up on his elbows so that not too much of his weight is on me.

My eyes drift shut. "You do."

"That's right. I do." He shifts onto one arm, using the other one to hold his erection at its base and move the head through my folds, paying particular attention to my clit.

Within a few seconds, I'm willing to beg him to fuck me. My breasts are heavy, my nipples tight, my womb aching for him.

"Tell me how much you want it," he practically purrs.

"I want it." My breath is labored.

"Who's the only one who can give it to you?"

"You are." Dante circles the head over my clit, and I moan, but it sounds almost like a sob to my ears. "You are, Dante. Please."

His cock shifts down and slowly pushes inside. He gives me a few moments to get used to the size of him, and when he's fully seated inside me, I gasp. I've never felt so full. Never knew I could.

When he shifts his hips and pulls out, pleasure like I've never known ricochets through my body. He thrusts back inside.

"You're so tight, tesoro. A perfect fit. Sei perfetta." He kisses my forehead then picks up the pace.

Within a minute, all traces of gentle, considerate Dante vanish.

The heels of my shoes dig into his lower back as he pounds into me, but he doesn't complain. With every push and pull, he drives me closer and closer to my climax.

The drag of his hard chest over my nipples is an exquisite torture I could become addicted to. Warmth floods my body, radiating out from my center and down my limbs, my skin coated in a fine sweat.

Dante pulls my left leg up so that the back of my thigh rests against his chest, my calf draped over his shoulder, and it changes the angle of his entry, making me cry out. Every time he pushes in, the feeling is so intense, I don't know what to do. It's like I want more of it, but I'm not sure I can handle more at the same time.

My fingernails dig into his shoulders as my head thrashes back and forth. I bite my bottom lip, trying to stem my urge to scream.

"That's it, let go. You look so good underneath me, taking my cock like a good little slut."

His words unravel me. I come apart, and I feel myself shuddering around his cock as my release reverberates through me. Dante brings his head into the curve of my neck while I ride out my orgasm.

"Fuck," he groans against my salty skin.

I don't have any time to recover. The instant my body is done clenching around him, he pulls out of me and flips me onto my stomach before hoisting me up by the hips. Using his knees, he spreads me wide so that he fits between my legs and pushes back into me.

I groan, arching my back. He's so deep like this.

Reaching forward, he grips what was once a bun, but I can feel it's now a ponytail, and he uses it to wrench my head back. The act strains the muscles in my back, but it's worth it because this feels like ownership, as though he's marking his territory and showing me who I belong to, and the truth is I don't hate it. Not at all.

"I'm gonna fuck you all the time now that I know what I'm missing, and you're going to let me, aren't you?"

"Yes!" I cry as he drags his cock out of me and slams back into me with a force that has me grunting.

Dante forces my face down to the mattress and brings one hand around between my legs. His fingers rub circles over my clit, and an orgasm bears down on me with an intensity that's almost frightening.

"No, I can't. I can't again."

But he doesn't stop. The feeling builds and builds until it feels as though I might explode, then I do. I shatter like a slingshot hitting a mirror, and tiny pieces of me scatter as I cry out his name.

"Fuck . . . yeeeees." With one final thrust, he holds himself inside me, and his cock jerks as he releases into the condom on a groan.

We stay still, panting until both of our releases subside, and we catch our breath. Dante pulls himself from me, and a small sound escapes me. I hear him make his way to the bathroom while I flop down onto the bed—sated, spent, and not sure what to do now.

Will he expect me to leave right away? Does he normally kick out his conquests, or do they stay the night?

I'm so deep in thought that I don't hear him return, and when he flops down beside me, I startle. He's on his back, one arm thrown over his head, and he brings the other one to rest on my ass, squeezing.

That's when I realize that I'm lounging around naked with him. I sit up to find my dress to cover myself, but he hauls me back down to his chest.

"Don't be shy now. Not after I already know what you taste like. Know what you sound like when you come."

My cheeks heat, and I push against his chest to get up again, but he won't let me move. We lie there quietly for a few minutes, and I listen as the cadence of his heart returns to a normal beat.

"Do you want me to go?" I ask awkwardly.

He squeezes me to him. "Hell no. We're just getting started."

"Oh. I didn't know if you usually ask girls to leave after or whatever . . ." What is my mouth saying, and why am I talking about other girls while I'm lying naked in his bed?

"I don't normally, no. But you're not some girl, you're my fiancée."

He says it as though that explains everything when really, a couple of months ago, I would have spit on this man if I'd found him dying on the sidewalk. Still, the words bring a warm feeling to my chest that most girls would probably fawn over, but that I can't help but see as a warning sign.

"What are you doing for the break between semesters?" he asks. His voice is a deep rumble in my ear pressed to his chest.

"Hadn't given it much thought. Just going back to New York, I guess. I was thinking of maybe asking Irina and Oksana if they wanted to go away somewhere hot for the week, but Irina can barely get out of my brother's bed these days, so I doubt she'd be up for it."

He shifts so that I'm no longer on his chest, and he's resting his head in the palm of his hand, looking down at me. "What would you think of coming back to California with me and spending the week there?"

I blink a few times, surprised. "I . . ."

I'm not sure what to say. I hadn't thought for a second he'd ever ask me. But the idea of getting away from home, with all its prying eyes and judgments, sounds ideal.

"Would we stay at your parents' place?"

He shrugs. "We could. I have my own space there. We also have a condo in downtown Los Angeles that we can stay in."

I think about it. It would be good to get an idea of the environment I'd be expected to live in once we're married. Maybe it would help me to decide on what to do about Sasha.

"How about we do both? I've never spent any time in California, and I'd like to do both."

Dante nods. "I'll make it happen. Just so you know though, Dom, Santino, and Bianca will be flying back with us, so if you're thinking we'll be banging on the plane . . ."

I roll my eyes. "I think I'll survive."

"You sure? I know my cock can be addicting." He tugs on my earlobe with his teeth.

I bat him away. "Sorry to disappoint."

"Well then, I guess my cock has to prove himself more." He rolls on top of me, both of us still naked.

I don't dare tell him what a liar I am.

CHAPTER TWENTY-THREE
DANTE

"I've been to your family home, and I know this isn't it. Where are we?" Polina asks from the passenger seat as the gates of the Malibu home open.

I shrug and pull my vintage Ford Bronco forward. "Changed my mind. I didn't want my mother listening to you come from the other side of the house."

She smacks me in the chest. "That's easily solved. No sex."

"I'm irresistible." I stop the car in front of the house. We own it, but no one in my family spends much time here. It's mostly me here in the summer when I want to surf.

Polina and I haven't slept together again since last Saturday night. She kept saying she had plans with her friends or that she had to study for her exams. I'm starting to think she was avoiding me.

But that comes to an end now. I have her all to myself for a week, and I plan to figure out what this could be between us. Because as against this as I was when I was first told I was going to have to marry her, my gut tells me there's something here.

But I have to trust her first. In order for us to get there, she needs to open up to me.

We get out of the Bronco, and I grab our bags from the back. After carrying them up the front steps, I set down one of the bags and punch in the code to unlock the door. Opening it, I motion for her to enter first.

She walks in past the foyer into the bright open space of the living room that's combined with the large kitchen. The ocean sits just out the bulletproof floor-to-ceiling windows across the back of the house, the sun low in the sky and sparkling on the water.

"Wow." She sounds genuinely impressed.

"C'mon. I've seen your family's brownstone. It has to have three times the square footage of this place."

Malibu beach houses aren't typically mansions. Not like our house in Calabasas.

She turns and faces me. "Maybe, but there's not an ocean view."

"True." I set the bags by the bottom of the stairs. "Bedrooms are upstairs, as is the gym."

She walks right up to the glass doors that lead out onto the spacious deck that has a bunch of lounge chairs, an eating area, and a hot tub. "Too bad it's not summer."

I walk up behind her. "We can still go in the hot tub, and when we surf, we just have to wear our wet suits."

She turns and looks at me in panic. "I don't surf, Dante."

"I'll teach you."

She shakes her head. "I don't think so."

I tuck a piece of hair behind her ear. "I wasn't asking. You'll have fun, trust me."

Polina looks as though she wants to say no, but she relents. "Fine. But if I see a fin in the water, or I almost drown, I'm done."

I laugh. "Deal."

"I want to check out the deck."

She unlocks and opens the door that leads outside, and I join her at the railing. When I told my dad of my plans, he said he'd have a security detail around to watch things. This time, on my turf, I don't feel as worried as I had been in New York.

The wind off the ocean whips her hair around, and the smell of the salt air immediately makes me feel at home. The sound of the waves reaching the beach is a backdrop to our conversation.

"It's so different than I'm used to," Polina says. I think it's more to herself than me, but I respond anyway.

"Could you see yourself liking it here?" It's not until the words are out of my mouth that I realize I genuinely care what her answer is.

She takes a moment before she speaks. "I think maybe I could."

I open my mouth to say something, but someone calling my name stops me. We both look to our left, and I see my neighbor out on his deck, smoking a joint.

I lift a hand in greeting. "Hey, man. How are you?"

"Good, good. Living the life." He puts what's left of his joint in the beer bottle in his other hand. "I'd invite you guys over for a beer, but I'm getting picked up. We're going to go try to catch some waves at Ocean Park."

"Next time." I wave again.

"For sure." He turns and goes back into his house.

Polina turns to me with wide eyes. "Was that . . ."

I nod and chuckle. "Yep." My neighbor is in one of the biggest bands in the country. "You know that actor James Crawford?"

She nods. "Yeah."

"He and his family live a few houses down."

"No way!" Her face lights up. "I love his movies."

I shrug. "Yeah, he's all right." My jealousy is shining through. "You want to unpack and then get something to eat? We're gonna have to get up early to go surfing tomorrow."

She groans. "You're really going to make me surf?"

I wrap my arms around her. "You know I love pushing your limits." I wink and open the door to the house, motioning for her to go first.

She may not be looking forward to it, but I'm hoping she enjoys herself tomorrow. Surfing is a big part of me, and it would be nice to be able to share it with the woman I'll be spending the rest of my life with.

* * *

POLINA WAS NOT happy when I forced her out of bed so early this morning to go hit the beach, especially since I kept her up half the night eating her pussy and pounding into her. Then when I got her into the wetsuit, and she figured out she'd be wearing the hood, booties, and gloves, she was even less thrilled.

But now that we're on the beach about twenty minutes away from my house, she's brightened up. It was cute as hell the way she concentrated and hung on every word I said when I was explaining to her the best way to try to get up on her board.

This morning, the waves are perfect for learning since there's not a big swell. She's attempted a few times to get up, and she's getting frustrated at her lack of progress.

"Just give it a try a few more times. You'll get the hang of it."

She rolls her eyes but agrees, clearly trying to appease me. This time she does manage to make it up on her board, but she gets excited and puts her hands above her head to cheer and falls. When she pops up, she's coughing and trying to catch her breath.

I swim over to her as fast as I can. "You okay?"

She nods, swallowing hard, eyes watering.

"You sure?"

"Yeah." Her voice is raspy. "But I think I'm going to go sit on the beach. I'd rather watch you do your thing. I've had enough for today."

I chuckle. "Okay. I won't be too long."

"Take your time, I'm happy to watch." She gives me a smile, the kind I thought I'd never see from her directed at me, before she swims away.

After catching a few sets of waves, I walk out of the water and over to Polina sitting on the beach, leaning back on her hands.

"You're really good," she says.

I sit beside her in the sand. "Been doing it most of my life. I try to get out here whenever I can."

"Well, it shows."

I knock my shoulder against hers. "Did I impress my fiancée?" I wink.

She shakes her head.

"Want to go dry off and change? Thought we could hit my favorite food truck on the way back. They have a killer crispy fish taco."

She shrugs. "Sure. I'm going to look like a hot mess, though."

I grab her hips and fall back into the sand, bringing her over me. Polina's usually so put together—perfect hair, perfect makeup, perfect outfit. And she's gorgeous, but I prefer this version of her. With no makeup on, her hair windblown and messy, she looks relaxed and open rather than guarded and closed off.

Without thinking, the truth slips from my lips. "You've never looked more beautiful."

I sit up and kiss her lips, holding her hips in my hands. She meets my gaze, and our eyes stare into one another's. I wish I knew what she was thinking. Is she thinking what I am? That I worry she's worming her way into my heart? I try to decipher her thoughts as neither of us says anything, but she gives me no sign. Eventually, she gives me a small smile and kisses me briefly before pushing off me and standing.

We peel off our wetsuits at the Bronco, quickly toweling dry before throwing on the clothes we brought over our swimsuits. No surprise, she brought a Gucci sweatsuit when I told her to bring something comfortable to change into. Always a fashionista.

The drive to the food truck takes about fifteen minutes, and after our order is passed off to us, we take a seat at one of the picnic tables set in the center of all the food trucks.

I moan when I first bite into my taco. "Fucking hell, I missed this."

Polina bites into hers and chews with a contemplative face, then swallows. "It is pretty good."

I scoff. "Pretty good. You can't tell me that New York City can produce fish tacos like this."

She smiles. "No, but you'll never find pizza here like you can in New York."

I could kiss the smug look off her face. "Touché. Next time we're there, you'll take me to your favorite place?"

"Yeah." She says the right word, but it doesn't sound as though she's so sure there will be a next time we're in New York together.

We eat in silence, both of us enjoying our meal.

"What was it like before your father died?" I ask. I've often wondered whether she was close to her father or if it was more of a "good riddance" situation when he passed, as I suspect it was for Marcelo when his father died.

She looks at the blue sky, the seagulls circling above, appearing a little wistful. "I was his only daughter, and he treated me like a princess my whole life. I could do no wrong. At least that's how it felt. He made me feel like he was proud of me just for breathing." A sad sort of smile tilts her lips.

"So that's why you're such a brat."

She crumples her napkin and throws it at me. I duck, and it sails over my shoulder.

I take her hand, and she doesn't fight me. "It must have been hard when he passed away."

She frowns and looks at our joined hands. "It was. I was pulled from class and brought home by one of my father's men. When

I got there, everyone was there—my mom, my brothers . . . they already knew. I remember thinking it couldn't be true." Her gaze flicks up to meet mine. "Because of what my father did, who he was . . . I always assumed he'd be killed, murdered by some faceless enemy I didn't know. I never suspected it would be something as mundane as a heart attack. That sounds awful, I mean—"

"I know what you mean." I squeeze her hand.

"When Feliks took over, things were pretty much the same for me. He was still so young and had so much to learn that he wasn't around a lot."

She pulls her hand from mine into her lap. We both know that even though I didn't pull the trigger that killed her brother, I played a role in everything that went down.

"Polina . . ." I'm not even sure what to say or how to broach this subject. "If things could have been different . . ."

She raises a hand and shakes her head, suggesting she doesn't want to get into it. "I get it. I know the way it goes. He kidnapped one of your own, and you had to get her back. I understand it, and I know he would have done the same had the roles been reversed. It's just hard sometimes . . . knowing you were there." Her eyes lift to mine, and her pain is evident. Is that why she's been keeping her distance from me? "I still don't even know why Feliks did it. When I ask, Dmitri will never tell me."

I don't know much except I owed Gabriele Vitale a favor, and he called it in that day. Feliks had Aria Costa, and Gabriele needed help getting her back. The Italians had to unify and show the Russians they couldn't take what was ours. If I'd known . . . no, the outcome would have been the same regardless of my involvement with Polina.

"I wasn't there when he was killed, just so you know." It's the truth. I can't say I didn't kill anyone that day, just not her brother. But she doesn't need to know that.

She nods and looks at her lap.

"I'm sorry." It's all I can really offer her. "Is it something you can get past?"

She sighs and looks at me. "I want to. I don't know if that's enough. I know it wasn't *you*, but it was your people, kind of."

I know what she means. It was the Vitales, Gabe to be precise, and though it's not like every family within the Italian Mafia is friends, we're certainly more aligned than we are with the Russians.

"I get it. But just know something, tesoro. If anyone ever took you from me—anyone, my people, your people, doesn't matter—I'd burn down the fucking world to get you back."

A nod is her only response, and I decide to change the subject.

"I figure we'll head to the condo in Los Angeles in a couple of days. That work for you?"

"What are we going to do when we're there?" she asks.

I shrug. "Whatever we want. I can take you shopping on Rodeo Drive in Beverly Hills. There are a few clubs we can check out at night if you want."

The smile is back on her face, which was my goal. I figured the mention of designer wear would do the trick.

CHAPTER TWENTY-FOUR
POLINA

The past few days with Dante have not been what I expected, mainly because I've enjoyed them. Enjoyed him and his company. I promised myself I'd go into this week with an open mind, just to see what it might be like between us if I didn't come at him with a constant attitude. Then when we return, I'll decide what to do about my original plan with Sasha.

Today we're leaving the Malibu house and driving to Los Angeles to stay at his family's condo downtown before we have to return to school.

Unlike after Christmas, I'm not looking forward to our return to Sicuro. I've loved being away from everything and everyone and having it just be the two of us. There's so much less pressure—I'm not wondering what everyone else is thinking when they see us together, I don't feel forced to have my walls up and act how other people expect me to, and I don't feel the divide that's wedged between Dante and me so prominently because of our different backgrounds. Here we're just two people enjoying each other's company.

"I have to make a quick pit stop before we reach Los Angeles."

I shift in the passenger seat to look at him. This is the first I'm hearing of this. "Where at?"

"I need to deliver something for my father. I won't be long."

That was my fear—it's family related. Enough said. I won't bother asking any more questions. He probably wouldn't tell me anyway. We're having fun, but I'm not sure he trusts me that much yet.

He pulls off the highway, and about five minutes later, we pull into the parking lot of an older stucco building that's been painted black and has a sign that says Misfits. There are no windows on the front of the building, just a set of double doors that lead inside. It's clearly a strip club. One I assume his family must own.

I have no judgment about it. My family certainly owns their fair share, and the women working there make good money. As long as they can do it on their terms, I see nothing wrong with dancing for cash. Still, that doesn't mean I'm thrilled Dante's going in there.

He unbuckles his seat belt and looks expectantly at me. "Let's go."

My eyebrows draw down. "I don't need to go in if you're just dropping something off."

"I'm not leaving you out here by yourself." He leans over and unbuckles my seat belt, bringing the scent of his cologne with him. As always, it makes me breathe deeper.

"I'm a big girl, Dante."

He brings one hand to my chin and forces me to look straight at him. "But you're my girl now, and I'm not leaving you here by yourself. People know you're my fiancée, and there are people who would love to take you away from me. I don't want you to end up like Aria Costa did last year."

Right, when my brother kidnapped her and ended up dead because of it.

"Fine." I push open the door.

He walks around the Bronco to meet me, taking my hand as we walk toward the entrance. Once he opens the door, the music playing for the girls on stage hits me like an invisible wall.

Dante keeps hold of my hand and greets the bouncer before leading me over to a booth in the far corner. He leans in so I can hear him over the music. "Stay here. I'll be back in a few minutes."

He exits the main room through a door on the side.

I watch for a few minutes as the waitresses make their rounds to the customers, and the strippers not on stage work the room, trying to procure a lap dance—or more, I'd guess, seeing that there's a sign at the far end for private rooms.

Dante comes back out of the door he went through and heads in my direction. But before he reaches me, a bleached-blond woman wearing a triangle bikini top and a super short schoolgirl skirt cuts him off. She places her hand on his chest, stepping into him. To his credit, he steps back and removes her hand, but she puts her hand into his hair, pressing her chest into his.

My hands fist in my lap, and I swear my pulse jolts in my neck. It's obvious to me they have history even if Dante is now forcing her off of him. Jealousy coats me like honey sliding from a jar.

She finally seems to get the hint and looks over at me, frowning. Then she gives me a smirk and a wink that makes me want to rush over and strangle her.

Dante makes his way to me, taking me in warily. I could try to hide the fact that I'm affected by what just went down, but I see no point. I know myself well enough to know that if I don't bring it up now, I'll stew about it until I lose it and it comes out anyway. Might as well get it over with.

He stands in front of me and holds his hand out to help me up, but when he tugs me to leave with him, I don't move. He turns back around, forehead creased.

"What was that all about?" I ask, loud enough so he can hear me over the music.

He steps closer to me so we don't have to shout to be heard. "I'm sure you figured it out, but I made it clear I wasn't interested. You saw that." Dante looks at me as though that should be the end of the conversation, but we both know that if the roles were reversed, there isn't a chance in hell he would just walk out of this club.

"So you've hooked up with her before?"

He seems to weigh his answer before he speaks. "Yes."

"When was the last time?" I don't know why I ask, why I feel this need to know.

A sheepish expression crosses his face. "She gave me a blow job the night I found out you and I were to be married." There is some guilt etched in his gorgeous features.

I'm enraged even if I know it's irrational. We had no relationship at the time, and I had no claim to him then. We hadn't even officially met yet. And it's not like I didn't already know that Dante messed around whenever he could before we were engaged.

Maybe it's because I haven't given him head yet, and she has. And I saw the way she looked at him. She wanted to do it again.

Dante's been so focused on pleasing me, and I've been happy to accept it. But there's zero chance I'm going to let this bitch feel as though she has one up on me.

I snag his hand, pulling him across the room.

"What are you doing?" he asks from behind me, but I don't slow down.

Not even when he tugs on my hand when I take us down the hall with the private rooms. The first door is closed but the next one is open, so I drag him in there.

"What the—"

"Shut up." I slam the door closed and lock it from the inside. I point at the black leather bench seat that runs in an L-shape in the room. "Sit."

He does as I say, looking at me warily.

The room is dimly lit, and there's a wide coffee table I imagine some of the girls dance on. The music from the other room is pumped in but at a much lower volume so we don't have to shout to be heard.

"Polina, what the hell are you doing? I know you're pissed, but—"

"Tell me, Dante, how mad would you be if some guy I gave a blow job to was all over me in front of you?" I lean in over him, running my nose up his neck. "How about imagining another man's dick in my mouth?"

His hands land on my hips. "Don't," he says through clenched teeth.

"Why not? She had her mouth on your cock. My cock." My hand slides down his body, and I rub his erection. "It's no different."

"Polina," he says as a warning.

"What? Don't you want me to be your good girl?"

I slide my body down, falling to my knees in front of him, and his eyes widen. When I undo his belt and his pants, his dick hardens more, making his arousal evident.

"Fuck, baby, you gonna suck me off?"

I thrill at the lust thickening his voice because I'm the one who's doing that to him, not her. Never her again.

Though I don't say anything, I pull his pants down a bit with his help and fist the base of his thick cock, which is answer enough.

"Wait." He puts his hand over himself. "Is this like a revenge blow job or something? You're not going to bite my dick off, are you?"

I look up at him from between his legs to see that he looks legitimately concerned. I lift his hands, and he allows me. "I'm going to make sure you forget every single blow job you've ever had before me."

His eyes soften with relief. "It's not a competiti . . . ahhh."

He doesn't finish his sentence because I trail my tongue from root to tip before gently sucking on the end of his cock. Dante's large, and I already know I won't be able to fit the whole thing in my mouth, but I'm determined to make him lose his mind.

I've only done this to one other guy in my life, but I've seen enough porn to know what I'm doing, I hope.

I bring my mouth over him and suck on the head, jerking the

base with my hand. When I swirl my tongue over the tip a few times, Dante's hands land in my hair, fisting the strands.

Once I feel as though I've driven him sufficiently crazy, I bob up and down on him, bringing him to the back of my throat until I gag and can't take anymore. He seems to like that. His hands tighten in my hair, and his hips come up off the seat to pump into my mouth. I keep moving up and down with my mouth and my hand, putting all my effort into it. When I glance up at Dante's face, his eyes have a fevered look, as if he's not in his right mind.

My inner sex kitten purrs at bringing out this side of him.

"You make me want to come already. Is that what you want, greedy girl?" His words are strained as though he's trying to hold back.

On my next swipe up, I come all the way off his dick, saliva dangling like a bridge between my mouth and his mushroom tip. "I want you to stand up and fuck my face. That's what I want."

I want him to use me, take what he wants from me, not deny himself any pleasure.

His nostrils flare, and he stands up straight away, then uses his hands in my hair to force my mouth back onto him. I go willingly, opening my mouth and trying to relax my throat.

"Look at you sucking on my cock like a little slut." He pistons his hips, dragging his cock in and out of my mouth.

My insides clench at his degrading words, and I want more of them. He doesn't disappoint.

"You're doing such a good job, tesoro. Fuuuck." He holds himself in my mouth, pushing as far as he can go, then a little further.

Just at the point where I feel like I can't breathe, he pulls me off him. I suck in huge gulps of air, my eyes watering, my chin covered in saliva. Then he shoves me back down again and does the same thing.

"You look so good like this, mouth full of my cock, eyes watering with tears running down your face. So beautiful." He pulls me off him again then puts me back on. "I can't wait any more. I need to come. You want me to come down your throat, don't you?"

I nod around the mouthful of his dick.

He pumps in and out of my mouth, thrusting his hips while he holds my head still. I imagine what we must look like, and I swear I almost come myself. His breaths become heavy and labored, and when he holds himself in my mouth one last time, he jets into the back of my throat. My throat works to swallow it all, my eyes meeting his hooded gaze.

Slowly, so slowly, he pulls his cock from between my lips, stroking my cheek with his thumb. "You are such a good girl."

I preen under his praise, feeling my chest expand. I wipe my chin with the back of my hand, then Dante helps me up. The moment I'm standing, he wraps his arms around me and brings his mouth to mine, kissing me, not caring if he tastes himself on my tongue. It's so hot.

When he pulls away, he uses his thumbs to brush the tear streaks off my face. When he's done, he rests his forehead on mine, keeping his hands on my face. "That was so fucking hot."

I chuckle, a buoyant feeling I'm not used to filling my chest. He sees a side of me no one has ever seen, and it feels good not to hide under that mask. To reveal myself and be accepted wholly by him.

It's then I realize I want more of this. More of us. More of him. If I can set aside my fear that Dante might be another man to bait and switch me, that is.

Still, as much as I want this, I don't know if I can have it.

CHAPTER TWENTY-FIVE
DANTE

It's getting late by the time we step out of the elevator into the penthouse condo in downtown Los Angeles. After the strip club where Polina blew my fucking mind, we stopped to get something to eat.

Now as we step into the condo, so different from the beach house and her family's brownstone in New York, I find myself waiting anxiously for her reaction. I'm as surprised as anyone that what she thinks matters to me. But it does. I want her to want to be out here with me when we're married.

Whether she picks downtown or closer to the ocean doesn't matter to me. I just want her to find someplace where she feels like she fits.

"What do you think?" I ask as she wanders around the space.

This is certainly the most masculine of my family's homes she's seen. The décor is contemporary with a lot of leather and shiny finishes scattered throughout. Rather than sharp angles, the furniture is curved on the edges with simple, solid fabrics.

"It's nice. Not really my style, but nice nonetheless." She steps to the windows to look at the glistening city below. "Not the same view as New York." She laughs.

Unable to keep my hands off her now that we've crossed into new territory, I step up behind her and lean my chin on her shoulder. "No, but which do you prefer? The beach house, being above the city here, or the views in Calabasas?"

She turns, wrapping her arms around my neck. Sometimes it's hard for me to believe how comfortable we are with each other now. "Why do you ask?"

"Because I need to know where to buy a house for my wife."

I love the little grin that transforms her face and makes her eyes sparkle. "I have some say in it?"

"Of course. It will be your home as much as mine. I want you to be happy."

She tilts her head and looks up at me. "Do you have a preference?"

I shrug one shoulder. "Not really. I've spent enough time all over, and they all have pros and cons. I want you to decide."

"Can I think about it?"

I pause, a part of me wondering if she means about me, about us and whether she can accept us enough to consider where we might live as a married couple. But it doesn't matter because we're getting married—and for the first time since I was told the news, I'm looking forward to it.

Even if Polina doesn't realize how good we can be together, I'm determined to prove it to her in time. No one is as surprised as I am by this revelation.

"Of course." I kiss her temple. "Should we go unpack in my bedroom?"

"Yes, I don't want that dress I'm wearing tomorrow night to get too wrinkled."

We're going to a nightclub tomorrow night. Polina was worried she wouldn't be able to get in because she's not twenty-one, but I assured her she'll have no problem—we own it. She's excited because there are often celebrities at the private tables, and she wants to see who she might recognize.

As I lead her down the hall, pulling our bags behind me, I don't tell her that she doesn't need to worry about the dress she brought because I have a surprise for her. If there's one thing that's been clear to me in the time I've spent with Polina, it's that she loves fashion. When we were relaxing at the beach house, she often thumbed through high-end fashion magazines, marking pages of the things she liked.

That's when I first got the idea, and since I have money and connections, I was able to pull off my surprise in short order.

I smile when I walk through the bedroom door and see that everything's been set up as I instructed. Bags and bags of designer goods are strewn around the room, filling the bed and part of the floor around it. Polina gasps behind me, and I let go of the suitcases and turn around to take in her reaction.

Her mouth hangs open, her eyes wide in surprise. "What is all this?"

"This is my present to you."

"But . . ." She walks farther into the room, her gaze sliding over all the designer names on the bags. "Why?" When she turns back to me, her face is maybe as soft as I've ever seen it, a genuine question in her eyes.

"Because I wanted to do something nice for you. Something I thought you might enjoy."

"I don't know what to say." She shakes her head as if she's stunned.

"You don't have to say anything. But you do have to model all of it for me. Especially the stuff in the La Perla bag." I grin.

She steps into me, her hand going to the hair at the back of my head. "I think that can be arranged." Her expression becomes less playful and more serious. "Thank you, Dante. It's been a long time since anyone has done anything like this for me. Not since my dad passed away."

I brush a piece of her blond hair behind her ear. "I know you can afford to go get all this stuff on your own, but I wanted to surprise you. Wanted to spoil you a bit."

Which is new to me. I've never once wanted to do anything like this for a woman.

"You did spoil me. Thank you." She steps away and undresses. "Maybe now I should show you how much I appreciate it."

"I think I'm going to like your brand of appreciation." I lick my lips.

Once she's fully naked, she walks over to the La Perla bag on the bed. "Let's see what's in this, shall we?"

But her bare ass is too tempting. She doesn't get a chance to try the lingerie on, because in seconds I have my pants undone, Polina bent over the bed, and I'm inside her.

After thoroughly showing Polina how much I appreciate her appreciation, we order some food and put on a movie. We're half chatting and eating our pizza and half watching the old action movie.

This is the side of Polina that has surprised me the most during our time here in California. The relaxed version of her in one of my T-shirts, hair pulled back with no makeup on, content to hang out and do nothing.

Before I got to know her, I think I pictured her sharpening her nails with a knife in her spare time.

"Do you think you'll miss New York when you move to the West Coast?" I ask around a bite of pizza.

"I'll miss the energy of the city sometimes, I think, but I will not miss the winters. Not even a little."

I chuckle. "How often do you think you'll want to go visit your family?"

Something darkens her expression, and she shrugs. "I don't know, we'll see."

This isn't the first time I've picked up on a weird vibe when her family is mentioned. "Do you think Pavel will end up marrying your friend Irina? I see them around campus together a lot."

She rolls her eyes. "Who knows? Those two are on and off constantly. It's been a while since they've been off, so I'm sure it's coming. I hope they don't end up together."

She seems to say the last sentence more to herself than to me. "How come?"

Polina looks as though she might not answer me at all, but in the end, she does. "Pavel can be a real jerk. Irina is my friend. I want better for her than that."

I want to ask a follow-up question, but I don't get the chance because she changes the subject.

"What do you think you would have done if this wasn't the life you were born into?" she asks.

I ponder, then shake my head. "No idea. This is all I've ever known. I'm good at what I do, so maybe I'm doing what I should be."

Her head tilts as if she's contemplating. "You know, you're different than I thought you'd be."

I chuckle, turning to face her completely. "Shoot. What did you think of me?"

"Domineering. Controlling. A prick who expected me to be seen and not heard."

"Is that what the men in your family are like?" I arch an eyebrow.

"Some of them, I guess."

"Same in the Italian families. But I've never been interested in sheltering away whoever I married, only to be pulled off the shelf and dusted off for events. God knows I'd fucking hate that. My job as your husband will be to keep you safe, but to me, that doesn't mean not allowing you to have a life."

She nods a bit absentmindedly, almost as though she's deep in thought. I watch as Polina takes another bite of pizza, and when she's done chewing, she looks at me. "I've been thinking about what you asked me. About what I might want to do after we're married . . ."

"And?"

She looks nervous to tell me, judging by the way she looks to the side for a beat. "You know I like fashion—obviously, based on my surprise. I thought it might be interesting to run my own fashion blog. Not like an influencer per se . . . though I'd be on socials. But have a newsletter I share weekly, maybe even give out fashion advice or help to style other people looking to elevate their game. I don't know; it's just an idea at this point."

"Would there be a way to do this without splashing your face and location all over social media?" Her security is my biggest concern, but unlike some guys I know, I'll never use it as an excuse to keep her under my thumb.

Her lips curl to the side as she thinks. "Yeah, I could do shoulders-down shots of my outfits of the day. There's no real reason why I ever have to show my face."

"Then you should do it if you think it will make you happy. Maybe wherever we buy, we can convert one of the rooms into a studio for you, so you have the proper lighting for your shots or your videos or whatever."

She beams at me, and it spurs this weird feeling in my chest, one I wasn't expecting.

"That would be amazing." She stares at me for a beat. "I still can't believe how different you are from what I was expecting."

"I could say the same about you."

She frowns.

"What?" I ask.

"I don't want to go back to the academy. I've enjoyed being away from everyone."

I know what she means. Having her all to myself has been amazing. "We have to return to the real world at some point."

"I know. I just wish we could hide away for a little longer."

I pull her onto my lap. "We'll still see each other at school. You need me, just say the word." I flex my hips into her ass.

She chuckles. "I guess. It just won't be the same."

I give her a chaste kiss. "No, it won't, but we won't be there forever. Only a few more months until the school year is done, then you can have me all to yourself if that's what you want."

She trails her fingertips down my face. "I think it might be."

Needless to say, we don't see the rest of the movie.

CHAPTER TWENTY-SIX

POLINA

We've only been back at school for a day and a half, and I already miss California. Miss being able to be with Dante in our own little world.

Now that we're back at the Sicuro Academy, it feels different. I ate at the Italian table last night and felt the most comfortable I have thus far, but I'm not going to walk into Roma House any time I feel like it, and he's not going to stroll in here to visit me.

Sure, he dragged me into the Roma House once, but that was different. I didn't have to look everyone in the eye, and almost no one was there—they were all at the Sadie Hawkins dance. And I left in the middle of the night when no one was up.

But we're meeting at the on-campus gym to work out together today, so I'm looking forward to watching Dante's muscles bunch and flex.

I head out of my room with my exercise gear on, a jacket slung over top. As I walk through the lounge area, Sasha spots me and calls my name. Though I managed to avoid him yesterday, it doesn't seem I'm that lucky today.

I still can't decide what to do about him. A huge part of me feels like a traitor for even considering following through with my original plan, but then I wonder if I'm being foolish and letting a good dicking steal my common sense.

"Hey," I say, trying to muster a smile for Sasha.

"Where are you headed? The gym?" He eyes what I'm wearing and the workout towel in my hand.

"Yeah. I was a bit of a sloth over break. Need to get back to it."

"Give me a second to change, and I'll go with you." He starts to walk past me, and I stop him with a hand on his arm.

"Actually, I'm meeting Dante there."

His expression goes blank. "How was your break with him? I was worried about you."

My heart stutters. If I'm going to push forward, this is where I'd tell him what an awful time I had, how I was scared he'd hurt me, how he disrespected me. All lies. I can't get the words out. I know they'd feel like acid in my mouth. Still, a part of me clings to my plan because by letting it go, I'd be acknowledging my growing feelings for Dante, my enemy, and that makes me feel like a fool. It's not as if he's professed his love for me or anything.

Dante did some really sweet things for me when we were away, there's no question, but that doesn't mean I can trust him with my heart. It doesn't mean he won't grow bored of me when he no longer views me as a challenge.

"It was interesting. I'll have to tell you about it some other time, though. I'm going to be late if I don't go outside to meet him, and I don't want to keep him waiting."

There, that's the truth while sounding ominous enough.

Sasha steps in closer. "Did you think about what I said?"

He knows I don't have to ask for clarification. "I didn't have a lot of time while I was away, but I will. Just give me some time."

He frowns. "We don't have that much time. Your brother is going to be walking you down the aisle in a few short months."

"We'll figure it out, okay? I just need to decide on the best way to deal with all this."

He doesn't look impressed, and I worry maybe he's onto me, but either way, I can't give him the answer he wants. I'm still trying to make sense of everything in my head.

"I'm sorry, I have to go. I'll catch up with you later, okay? Promise."

He nods, and I leave, knowing Dante will be outside to meet me any moment. I step out into the dark and cold to wait. He's usually pretty prompt, so I'm sure he'll be here any minute.

The door opens behind me. I turn to see who it is and freeze when I see Pavel. I can tell instantly that this won't be a pleasant visit. Ever since the first time he came to me angry in my bedroom when we were kids, I've had an innate sense of when it was going to be bad. It's been a long time since he visited me for his sick purposes, though, and a part of me had hoped he'd changed, even though I knew he hadn't.

Pavel grips my wrist—hard—and drags me away from the door. He leads me along the front of the building, then off the path. I struggle to get out of his hold, but he only grips my wrist harder, and a pained sound leaves my mouth.

The small smirk on his face over the fact that he's hurting me makes me stop struggling. I've learned over the years that it's best to shore up my defenses and pretend he's not hurting me because he gets some kind of sick pleasure from seeing me in pain. Whenever he gets like this, I try not to show him how much he's hurting me.

Once we're around the side of the building, he finally comes to a stop. "How was your little getaway? It was all Dmitri could talk about while we were on break."

At least now I know where this is coming from. Pavel has never taken well to me getting any type of attention or praise.

"It was fine." I rip my wrist from his grasp, and this time, he lets me.

"Just fine?" He arches an eyebrow and gives me a disgusted look.

"Why do you care?" I cross my arms.

"Haven't you heard? Apparently, the fate of our well-being as a crime family rests on your shoulders. We're all looking to you as our savior." He practically spits out the words.

"It's not like I wanted to be in this position. You're acting like I'm relishing being in it. I was forced into it. I was happy just living my life."

A caustic laugh leaves his lips. "Oh yes, our little Bratva princess, living life without a care in the world. Never contributing anything to the family other than her looks and ability to procreate. So sorry that you were called to contribute for once."

My temper finally gets the better of me. "Would you listen to yourself? First, you're pissed off that I'm getting attention for the role I have to play, the only role I have in this family, and then you're mad that I wasn't excited about it."

I should know better by now. I know how Pavel reacts when I talk back to him in these moments.

His hand jerks out and forms an iron grip around my upper arm. Even through my coat, it feels as if he's crushing my bones together. There's an unhinged glaze over his eyes that scares me.

"You think you're so much better, smarter than I am. You always have." His grip grows even stronger, and I whimper, unshed tears stinging my eyes. "When really, you're just a useless piece of skin. You don't do anything for this family, never have. You'll fuck up this thing with Dante, I have no doubt, because all you ever think about is yourself."

I cry out when he presses even harder, studying me for my reaction. It feels as though my bone breaks under his grip, and the first tear falls. A satisfied gleam enters his eyes. He's always loved to push me until I break.

"I have to go. Dante will be waiting for me." I barely get the words out through the pain, but it's the only thing I can think of to get him to let me go.

Pavel's nostrils flare, and he drops his hand from my arm.

I don't wait for him to change his mind, spinning and going back the way I came while brushing tears from my face with my other hand. The one on the arm that isn't throbbing right now and almost hurts as much as when Pavel still gripped it.

His footsteps sound behind me, and I pick up the pace. When I come around the corner, Dante is waiting in front of the building for me.

He spots me and smiles, but I must not be as good an actress as I think I am at covering up my distress because his smile is replaced with concern. His gaze darts over my shoulder, and I know he's watching my brother emerge from behind me.

Inhaling a deep breath, I walk straight up to Dante. "Ready to go?" I ask with a smile I'm sure doesn't reach my eyes.

"Yeah." He doesn't remove his gaze from my brother, watching him until he goes back into Moskva House. "Everything okay?"

"Of course. Let's go get a sweat on." I walk in the direction of the gym, and Dante follows, though I get the feeling he doesn't believe me.

Any made man worth his name would know I was lying.

CHAPTER TWENTY-SEVEN
DANTE

I don't care what Polina says, something went down between her and her brother. She clearly doesn't want to discuss it because she's pretending like she's fine, even though she's very clearly not.

When we arrived in the gym, she opted to go over to the treadmill. I don't know if that's because she always likes to start her workouts on the treadmill, or if she wanted to be away from me so she could compose herself to better sell her story that she's fine.

But I'm like a bloodhound now, and I'm going to follow this scent until I track down the truth. That said, I'll give her a little space for the time being because if I push her before she's ready, she'll close up, and I'll be left trying to pry the door open with a butter knife.

I do my own thing, and eventually, she comes over and joins me. Her hair is pulled back in a ponytail, and she wears leggings that show off every perfect curve on her body. On her top, I assume she's wearing a sports bra, but I can't tell because she has on a thin zip-up athletic sweater.

"You want to lift some weights with me?" I ask.

She hesitates. "Yeah, okay. Nothing too heavy, though. My arms are still sore from yesterday."

I pause. I didn't know she came here yesterday. She didn't mention it. Not that she has to report to me with what she does every second of her day. Brushing aside my concern, I grab a set of tens and bring them over to her.

"What's your favorite exercise to do?" she asks as she takes them.

"Probably shoulder presses."

Her gaze skims my muscled shoulders, visible in the tank I'm wearing, and her lids droop.

I lean in and whisper into her ear, "Don't go looking at me like that, or you're likely to find yourself in one of the combat rooms, riding my dick."

She licks her lips as I pull away.

"Let's do them together."

I notice the tightness around her eyes and jaw every time she has to bring the weights up, so I set down mine and step closer to check her form.

"Here, just bring your arms a little more—" I touch her upper arm to move it and demonstrate where it should be, and she flinches, her eyes squeezing shut and the weight dropping to the floor in a loud thump.

"Sorry." Her face is red as she shakes.

"What's wrong? Is your arm sore?" My forehead wrinkles.

"It's nothing. Sorry, you just startled me."

I frown. She's lying.

"Come with me." I take the other weight from her hand and set it on the floor, then link my hand with hers and lead her to one of the combat rooms.

The rooms are private so that no one can see you practice your fighting technique. The last thing you want is for your enemy to be taking notes.

Once we're inside, I close the door and turn to face her, arms crossed. "Take off your sweater."

It's clear from my tone that it's not a request, and her head rears back.

"What? What are you talking about?"

"Take off the sweater. I want to see what's under there."

If I were an animal, I would be able to smell her fear right now. Her eyes are wide, her expression panicked, and her gaze darts to the door as though she's about to bolt.

"I don't want to take off my sweater. I'll be cold." She lifts her chin in defiance.

"You can put it right back on after I get a look." I step closer. "Now. Take. Off. Your. Sweater."

Her face twists in fury, and she stomps toward the door. "I don't know what this is about, but I'm not playing this stupid game with you."

I shift to the side to stand in front of her. When she tries again, I step to the other side.

She blows out a breath of frustration. "Would you just let me leave?"

"After you take off your sweater. You can do it, or I can do it for you. Your choice." I meet her gaze and hold it. She holds a cutting stare, but I don't so much as blink.

Tears well in her eyes and a ragged "Fine" slips from her lips. Slowly, she drags down the zipper of her sweater. Then she pulls her right arm out of the sleeve and finally, almost reluctantly, she pulls out her left arm.

On her left arm are what appear to be new bruises forming in the shape of fingertips.

Someone is a fucking dead man.

It takes me a minute to say anything as I attempt to gather my rage so that I don't scare Polina. I know whatever happened to her has to have been upsetting to her, and I don't want to do any more damage by going off. It takes longer than I'd like as I stare at those bruises—it's not in my nature to rein myself in, but I have to for her sake.

"Who?" My voice is low, close to a whisper. I'm afraid if I speak any louder, I'll roar like a dragon.

Even more tears well in her eyes until she blinks, and one slips free. It fucking kills me to watch this strong woman who pretends like nothing affects her cry.

"Who, Polina?"

She shakes her head and turns away from me. "I can't tell you." Her voice is so quiet I almost can't make out the words.

I move behind her, my front to her back as I hold her. "Tesoro, someone hurt you. If you think there's any possibility I'm not going to dole out retribution, you're insane. No one hurts what's mine. You are the woman who is to be my wife, and no one gets away with hurting you."

For whatever reason, she cries even harder. She wraps her arms around herself and drops her chin to her chest, shaking as she sobs.

I have to suck in a deep breath through my nose. Every instinct in me is roaring to haul ass out of here and track down who did this, even if I have to scour the entire campus and leave destruction in my wake.

I turn her around to cradle her in my arms, pressing a kiss to the top of her head. "The only way I can protect you is if you tell me, tesoro." She cries harder, and I place my finger and thumb on her chin, lifting so she looks at me. "Who hurt you? Was it Sasha?"

He was my first thought. Maybe he got pissed off that she rejected him.

She shakes her head. "It wasn't him."

"If you're lying to protect him—"

"I swear, I'm not."

I lead her to the edge of the room and take a seat, leaning against the wall, and pull her into my lap. "Then who?"

She meets my gaze for the first time in minutes. "You have to promise me you won't do anything if I tell you."

I scoff. "I can't promise that, and you know it."

She expects me to look at what someone did to her skin and do nothing about it? Not a chance in hell.

"Please, Dante." She grips my tank top. "Promise."

My teeth grind together. I need to know who it was, but there's no chance I'll be able to stop myself from making them pay for hurting her. I don't want to lie to her. I consider myself above lying. I'll tell people what they don't want to hear to their face. But in this instance, the lie is worth it.

"Fine," I grind out.

"Pavel," she whispers, burying her head in my chest.

I swallow back my rage. "Has he done this to you before?"

I know the answer even before she nods, still looking at her lap.

I tilt her chin up, searching her gaze. "Why?"

Her shoulders sag. "I don't know. I really don't. I used to think it was because he was jealous, but as I got older, I started to wonder if maybe there was something seriously wrong with him. He takes pleasure in hurting me."

I inhale another deep breath through my nose in an attempt to bring down my heart rate. "What do you mean as you got older? How long has this been going on?"

Her lips press together. "It started when we were nine. The first time he came into my room. He was angry about something. I don't even remember what, just that it had nothing to do with me. When I tried to calm him down, he took my arm and bent it behind my back. He almost popped my shoulder out. Might have if my mother hadn't knocked on the door. When she asked why I was crying, I lied and said that I was upset about something else."

"Why did you lie for him?" I brush a piece of hair that's fallen from her ponytail behind her ear.

"I don't know. Because he's my twin? I didn't know at the time that it was the beginning of a pattern."

"How often does it happen?"

She shrugs—with her good arm, I note. "There's no rhyme or reason to it. It only got worse as the years went on. He got more and more jealous of me, for some reason, and how much he hurt me and how often it happened escalated. Once he pushed me down the stairs, and I broke my arm. I lied and said I slipped. He used to burn me with cigarettes when we were in our teens. Right here on my side. He'd do it in the same spot every time so I'd only ever have the one scar, and no one could see it unless I was undressed. He'd hold me down and . . ." She squeezes her eyes shut.

I know the scar she's talking about, I've seen it, and the knowledge of where it came from makes my chest ache. It would be easy to dig into her about why she continued to lie for him, but this isn't on her; it's on him. She's done nothing wrong, and I know without asking that she's afraid of him, probably afraid of what he'd do if she ever told anyone. That's likely why she made me promise not to do anything.

"Do you know how hard it was growing up listening to people say how lucky I was to be a twin, how amazing it must be to have someone look out for me, how close we must be, all the while knowing how cruel Pavel was? How much pleasure he took in my pain?"

I wrap her in my arms and pull her into my chest, slowly rubbing my hand up and down her back. "No one's ever going to hurt you again now that I'm a part of your life, you understand? No one."

She pulls away and looks at me, wide-eyed. "You can't say anything, Dante. You promised."

"Does Dmitri know?" I've seen the way he looks at his younger sister, and it would surprise me if he did and let it go on. I imagine someone doing that to my baby sister and know without a doubt I would kill them by torturing them slowly.

She shakes her head. "You're the only one I've ever told."

I rest my forehead on hers, wanting to wrap her up and protect her from anything and anyone that might dare to hurt her. "I'm going to take care of you now, understand?"

She nods against my forehead.

"I don't want you alone around Pavel anymore, under any circumstances, okay?"

"I already try to avoid that."

"If you find yourself alone with him, I want you to leave immediately. We only have a few months left of school, and then you won't have to be around him again. You're coming with me to California as soon as school is done."

She pulls back and looks me in the eyes. "Before our wedding this summer?"

"Yes. If you think for one second I'm going to let you go back to living in that brownstone with him, knowing what he's doing to you, then you don't know me. Don't fight me on this, Polina; it's nonnegotiable."

"All right." She wraps her arms around me. "Thank you."

"What for?" I squeeze her tightly.

"For being the only person these days who seems interested in protecting me."

I pull back so I can look her in the eyes. "I will always protect you." *Even if that means doing something you don't want me to,* I don't add. "Now, let's go get some arnica cream for you from the campus store. It will help it heal a little faster."

She nods. "Okay."

Polina stands, and I join her.

"You realize everyone's going to think we were fucking in here, right?"

My comment lightens the mood, as I'd hoped it would.

She laughs. "Maybe. Though we were pretty quick, so I'm not sure that's saying much about you."

My hands go to her hips, and I tickle her. "Watch out, next time

I'll lock you in here for twice the amount of time and make sure everyone hears your screams of pleasure."

She shakes her head, squirming out of my hold, laughing. "Promises," she says, and our eyes lock. "Thank you, Dante."

I pick up her sweater and step closer to her, running my thumb along the lone tear slipping. "You never have to thank me."

She smiles and seems in better spirits now, more relaxed.

I almost feel bad for lying about what I have planned for her brother.

* * *

ANOTHER WEEK PASSES before I get the opportunity I've been waiting for. I'm walking by Moskva House, and Pavel steps out ahead of me on the path—alone.

I pick up my pace so that I gain on him without drawing his attention. It's not until I'm almost on him that he turns to look over his shoulder. Wrapping my arms around him from behind, I drag him off the path and to the corner of Dublin House—the dorm for all the Irish kids.

He fights me, but I'm taller and stronger. Little does he know I want him to fight me. I'll take any excuse I can get to put my hands on this stronzo.

Once we're all the way at the side of the building, the same kind of place where he targeted my fiancée, I push him against the wall. He manages to get his hands out just in time so his face doesn't smash against the brick. Then he whirls around, his face a portrait of rage.

"What the fuck do you think you're doing?" he spits, stepping up to me.

I push his chest so he stumbles back against the building. "Delivering you a warning—if you put your hands on Polina again, I'll cut them off. That's not me being poetic either, asshole. I will steal a butcher's knife from the kitchen, find a saw, whatever, and I will remove your hands from your body. Don't lay a fucking finger on her again. Better yet don't even breathe in her direction, capisce?"

My hands are fisted at my sides in what I consider a valiant effort not to connect them with his face.

"I don't know what she told you, but she's full of shit."

I step toward him, and he's smart enough to step back until his back rests against the wall. "I saw the bruises on her arm, and you're lucky I'm not slitting your throat right now. The only reason I'm not is because your sister asked me not to say anything. I think she'd be really pissed at me if I killed you."

He smartly doesn't say anything in response even though I wish he'd run his mouth to give me an excuse to pop off. Instead, he stands there glaring at me as though he'd like to kill me as much as I'd like to kill him.

Fuck it.

I swing and hit him in the face, enjoying the burn on my knuckles.

He bends at the waist, holding his face. "Fuck you."

"Keep this between the two of us unless you want it to get out that you like to hurt women—your twin sister at that." And I turn and leave.

Because I feel the monster getting ready to rage inside me, and I have plans. I told Polina to meet me at the abandoned caretaker's house. I have a whole thing already set up for us, and as much as I'd like to strangle the life out of this guy, it's been too long since I've been with her.

Everyone thinks that because I'm usually easygoing and affable—at least compared to a lot of guys in this life—there's no part of me that's violent and cruel. They couldn't be more wrong. It just takes someone to flip that switch, and Pavel definitely flipped it. It's a testament to my feelings for Polina that he's still breathing.

I was already out at the caretaker's house earlier today to drop off everything we'd need for tonight, knowing no one would be out there. It's only used for parties on the weekends.

Once I reach it, I go straight upstairs to where I left everything. It remained untouched in my absence. God, I can barely wait for her to get here. It's been too long since she's been naked and writhing under me.

CHAPTER TWENTY-EIGHT
POLINA

I have no idea why Dante wanted me to meet him at the abandoned caretaker's home. He refused to tell me, but as I stepped over the threshold into the quiet dark of the house, I wondered if coming here was a smart idea.

"Dante?"

"Up here," he calls from the second floor.

I take the stairs up to the second floor. An orange glow comes from the room at the end of the hallway.

"Dante?" I ask again, taking baby steps in that direction.

"In here," he coaxes.

I follow his voice toward the room, and when I reach the doorway, I gasp. Dispersed throughout the room are all kinds of lit candles. It's cool outside, and therefore in here, but with candles burning, it feels warmer. The orangey-yellow glow warms the space and flickers on the walls.

In the center of the room is a makeshift bed with piles and piles of blankets, and on top of them is Dante, stripped except for his boxer briefs.

"It felt impolite to be waiting with my cock out." He shrugs, and I laugh.

"What's all this?" I step into the room.

He pats the spot in front of him on the bed, and I step over to join him. As soon as I do, he brushes my hair over my shoulder and removes my coat.

"It's been too long since I've been inside you. Since neither of us really wants to go into the other's dorm, I figured this could be our secret meeting spot. What do you think?"

I glance around at all the effort he's put into this. "I think you're a closet romantic."

His deep chuckle reverberates through the empty room. "Yeah, my secret is safe with you."

Once my jacket is off, he starts in on my shirt, lifting it over my head, then pressing a kiss to the nape of my neck. My head falls back, giving him better access while his hand roams, finding the clip to my bra in the center of my chest and pressing it so my breasts spring free.

He slides the straps of my bra down my arms, then gently lowers me onto the blankets where he worships my chest. Dante licks and nips, suckles and soothes, making me so desperate to have him inside me that I arch my back and gyrate my hips, looking for any kind of friction from where his hips are wedged between my legs.

He pushes my breasts together with his hands and chuckles as he runs his tongue back and forth from one nipple to the other. "So impatient." Then he clicks his tongue.

My hands delve into his hair. "Dante, please."

He bites my nipple, and I cry out. "I love it when you say my name like that, tesoro."

Finally, he makes his way down my body, trailing his tongue as he goes. When he reaches the top of my jeans, he passes them by. I almost protest until I realize that he's working his way down to my shoes to get them off first.

Once he's tossed aside my shoes and socks, he comes back up to undo my jeans before he strips me of them and my underwear. I lie there completely bared to him while his heated gaze roams over my body. When he continues to stare at me, I can't help but move around, needing his hands on me, his tongue—anything.

His hands take my knees, and he spreads me wide before bending down and swiping up from my entrance. He meets my gaze, his eyes reminding me of some jungle cat about to feast on dinner. He even licks his lips.

"You always taste so good." Then he settles between my legs.

His tongue delves between my folds, and he pushes two fingers into me. The sound in this quiet space as he eats me out is vulgar in the best way. He doesn't take his time or go gently. He's like a man possessed, intent on making me climax as fast and as hard as possible.

It doesn't take long before my hands are in his hair, and my thighs are pressed to the sides of his head while I arch off the floor, coming on a cry of his name.

It takes me a minute to recover, and when I come back, I find Dante lying beside me on the blanket, boxer briefs long gone, and his solid length straining. I want to return the favor, so I sit up and position myself on my hands and knees beside him, taking him in my grip.

"I want that, believe me I do, but right now, I need to be inside you. I've just tasted you, now I want to feel you." He sits up and grabs me under my arms, dragging me up and over until I'm straddling him.

His rigid length is now below me and between my folds, and it's instinctual to grind down on him, spreading my arousal all over him.

He groans and takes my hips in his hands, lifting me a bit. "Sink down on it, tesoro."

Gripping the base, I do as he says, slowly enveloping him. Once he's fully seated inside me, I am still, enjoying the feeling of him stretching me. As I rock back and forth, up and down, one of his hands goes to my hip and the other to my breast, which he gently palms.

Dante did indeed see a doctor while we were in California, and he's been bare inside me ever since. The sensation of feeling him skin to skin almost feels like too much every time he slides into me. It makes our connection that much deeper.

I set a steady but unhurried pace, looking down at him while he watches where we're joined.

"Just like that, just like that," he says in a soft, raspy voice.

My orgasm builds ever so slowly.

The candlelight flickers on both our bodies, softening the scene. There's no praise or derogatory talk tonight, but I don't miss it because this is something different. Something that feels weighted with emotion.

When I'm close, I grind my hips down against him over and over. Dante palms the back of my neck and pulls me down so my face hovers a few inches from his. We watch one another intently as the need to come swells up inside me, overtaking every thought, then I'm coming.

My eyes close, and my hips jerk, and I'm overwhelmed by both pleasure and emotion.

Dante rolls us so that he's on top while my core still clenches around his cock. When I can, I open my eyes and stare at him, so intense as he looks down at me. He comes all the way down and kisses me, deep and thorough as though he's pouring all of his emotions into that kiss.

When he pulls away, he moves with a slow and steady pace. He kisses my forehead, the end of my nose, my cheeks, my jawline, showing more softness and reverence than I could have ever thought he was capable of. Some foreign feeling swells in my chest, and I can't get close enough to him. I wrap my arms around him and pull him to me. He tucks his face in my neck.

"Polina, fuck, you're everything to me." Then he groans long and hard and spills himself inside me.

We lay there for a while, our bodies joined as he softens inside my body. Our hearts beat, chest to chest, in the same rhythm, slowing as we catch our breath.

Tears prick my eyes as I stroke his back with soft passes of my fingers. To think that if I hadn't given him a chance, I would have missed out on this. I'd never have known what lies under the façade of the easygoing playboy with poor impulse control. Certainly more than I ever would have suspected.

He pulls back and kisses me slowly, and I try to pour every single emotion I'm feeling right now into that kiss. His gaze bores into mine when we break off.

I can tell from his gaze that he knows as well as I do that something has shifted between us, and when I look up at him, I know I'll be calling Sasha off. I will be committing my life to this man, for better or worse.

* * *

I TEXT SASHA the next evening and ask him to stop by my room so we can talk. It might not be the smartest move, but it's the only place we'll have privacy, and I truly don't know how he'll react. I can't chance my original plan getting back to Dante. It will ruin everything we've built.

Besides, it's not as if Dante is going to walk into Moskva House and knock on my door while Sasha is here.

The sound feels ominous.

I swing open the door with a nervous smile and startle when I see Sasha *and* Pavel talking.

What is Pavel doing with Sasha?

Pavel has been quieter than usual around me. He doesn't say anything, but he still glares at me. I'll be so happy when I no longer have to be around him.

Sasha turns toward me. "Hey."

"What are you doing here?" I ask my brother.

His expression is blank. "I was leaving Irina's room, ran into Sasha, and we started talking. Problem?" He lifts his brow in challenge.

"Of course not, just curious." I feign nonchalance, but I'm not sure my act is believable.

"Yeah, me, too." He looks between Sasha and me. "Well, I gotta go see Dmitri about something. See you guys later."

Pavel heads down the hall toward the elevator while I take a calming breath and relax.

"You all right?" Sasha walks into my room, and I shut the door behind him.

"Yep, fine. Thanks for coming." I motion for him to sit on the couch.

He does, and I remain standing.

"I assume you have me here because you thought about my suggestion?" He looks at me expectantly, with hope in his eyes.

I feel like the world's biggest bitch for leading him on and for even thinking about manipulating him to kill Dante. "I did."

"I've been thinking of how it might be done to look like an accident so that no one points their finger at either of us."

I blow out a breath, my stomach rebelling with my nerves. "I don't think that will be necessary."

A deep line forms above the bridge of Sasha's nose. "What do you mean?" He stands and walks over to me.

"I don't want anything to happen to Dante. Now that I've gotten to know him better . . . I don't want out of the engagement."

Sasha looks at me as if I'm speaking another language. "Wait, you're serious?"

I nod, playing with my fingers in front of me.

"What about us?" His gaze searches my face.

This is where I have to decide whether to come fully clean or not. I'm not sure what I should do. I don't want to hurt him any more than I already have, so I opt to pretend my feelings for Sasha just aren't as strong as my feelings for Dante. Telling him I was using him and lying to him from the start will only hurt him more, and I've done enough damage.

"As I've gotten to know Dante, I've realized that he's not who I thought he was. I've come to care about him."

Sasha scowls at me, his face red. "And you don't care for me anymore? You're just tossing what we might have to the side?"

"I'm not trying to hurt you, Sasha."

He steps forward, and I flinch, a reaction bred into me from my interactions over the years with an angry Pavel. But he doesn't notice, or if he does, he ignores it, taking my shoulders in his hands.

"You can't be seriously thinking of trusting him? Dante Accardi? He's a whore and a fucking Italian. He'll always put them over you. If we were together, you know how much easier it would be for us to exist in the world. Tell me you're not that naïve, Polina."

His insidious words worm into my brain, finding the weak spots where I haven't shored up my defenses against this kind of thinking. Maybe Dante is just another Pavel lying in wait.

No. He's not. I saw the way he looked at me the night we made love. You can't fake that.

"You can think what you want, but I'm not naïve." I shrug off his hold on me. "I'm sorry if you're upset, but this is what I want."

He spears me with a glare. "You're going to regret it. Mark my words. One day, you'll regret that you didn't choose me."

No, I won't. But I don't tell him that.

He walks to the door, muttering in Russian, and doesn't look back at me when he leaves.

That went about as well as expected. I didn't enjoy doing it, but I feel lighter now that it's done and not hanging over my head like a guillotine.

Now I can really move forward with my life with Dante. I consider it a fresh start, even if I'm the only one who knows it.

CHAPTER TWENTY-NINE
DANTE

I don't know what it is, but something about Polina has seemed . . . carefree the past couple of weeks. She remains somewhat stoic in public and doesn't say much, but a little of the ice that surrounds her has melted away. She's even comfortable holding my hand on campus, and she regularly eats meals at my table, slowly making conversation with more and more of the people at the Accardi table.

From what I can tell, Pavel is keeping his distance from her. The odd time she does sit in the Aminoff section of the dining hall with her friends Irina and Oksana, he doesn't talk to her or even look in her direction.

That Sasha guy though, he's another story. He's always stealing looks at my fiancée, sometimes ones that make me think he wants to fuck her and other times ones that look like he wants to strangle her.

And I don't fucking like it.

So when the opportunity presents itself for me to go head-to-head with him in our combat class, I pounce on it like a panther.

"I need a volunteer to spar with Sasha," Mr. Smith says, looking around the room.

I step forward before someone else can. Usually, Mr. Smith pits Russians against Russians, Italians against Italians, and so on. Less chance of things getting out of hand, I figure. But he looks between the two of us and, for whatever reason, gives me a nod.

I step into the center of the ring while the murmurs around us start up.

"Remember this is sparring, not combat. The point is to make contact using the techniques I've been teaching you, not beat the shit out of each other," Mr. Smith says. He stands between us and gives us a warning glare.

Sure, I know the rules. But it's not uncommon for someone to accidentally connect with another person from time to time. No one's perfect.

We each nod at Mr. Smith to signal that we understand, but I can tell from the hatred in the glare Sasha is directing my way that he has no plans to abide by the rules. Mr. Smith signals for us to begin, and we start with the usual circling around, hands raised, feet deft. We're both sizing up our prey.

There's no doubt in my mind that at some point, Sasha wanted Polina to be his. I saw them at that party together. So whether that's why he hates me or if it's just because I'm Italian and marrying a Russian bride, I have no idea. Nor do I give one shit. This is my opportunity to show this guy that I am not to be fucked with since he doesn't already seem to know.

I allow him to throw the first punch, easily shifting out of the way. His mouth tightens. Oh, he didn't like that, so I give him a grin that's sure to get further under his skin. Guys always make mistakes when they allow themselves to become irritated. They're less patient and make moves they shouldn't.

He attempts to hit me on the other side, and again I dodge his fist. I can do this all day, but I'm getting kind of bored, so I decide to move things along.

I strike and connect with his shoulder. Not hard, not yet. Just doing it the way I'm supposed to in class. He needs to be the first one to break so that I have a reasonable defense.

All the guys surrounding us shout and cheer, a mix of English, Italian, and Russian words thrown out at us.

Sasha tries to kick me, but I bounce back out of the way. The next time he tries to do that, I'm going to grab his leg and put him on his ass. I strike with my less dominant arm, something he doesn't seem to be expecting, and hit him square in his chest.

A low sort of snarl rips out of him, and I chuckle. His face grows red, and he grits his teeth, swiping at me with his fist again. But I manage to dodge it at the last second.

There's laughter in the crowd—at him, I suppose, for looking so fucking pathetic.

That really pisses him off, judging by the fury that transforms his face. When he swings this time, I let him hit me in the face. And I laugh.

I've always liked to let the other guy get a hit in. I don't know why. It's like an adrenaline shot to my system, and it always gets me more riled up and ready to kick some ass. Sasha's hit to my face is no different. Especially when blood trickles down from the corner of my eyebrow.

I smile widely at him, probably looking like a bit of a psycho before I move in. I need to act fast in case Mr. Smith decides to put an end to this session. I'm surprised he hasn't already, given that Sasha drew blood. But maybe he can see we have unspoken things to work out and thinks it's better this way than outside these walls where we're left to our own violent urges.

I snap out my fist and nail him in the stomach, causing him to hunch over when he loses his breath. Then I swipe his feet out from under him so that he falls on his back.

Cheers and jeers fill the room as I pounce on top of him, straddling his chest and raining hellfire down on him. Faster than hummingbird wings, my fists hit his face—one, two, three, four. On the fifth, I finally feel hands around my arms and shoulders to haul me off him.

Using all my strength, I lean down over Sasha so my mouth is near his ear. "Stay the fuck away from my fiancée. Consider this your only warning."

I allow myself to be hauled off Sasha, who spits blood onto the floor.

Santino looks just as psyched as I am, grinning from ear to ear. "Nice job, cuz. Don't know what that was about, but I liked it."

Mr. Smith pushes Santino to the side and steps in front of me. "I hope whatever issues you two have with each other, you've both managed to get it out of your system." He turns to face the room as a whole. "And I trust that what happened here will remain between all of us and not make it to the ears of the administration."

Everyone nods in agreement, no one wanting to be labeled a rat.

One of the Russians helps Sasha up, and I grin at him while he glares in my direction.

Mr. Smith directs his attention back to me and grips my shoulder. "You good now?"

"Peachy." I smile, tasting a bit of the blood that must have trickled from my eyebrow down into my mouth.

"Come get a first aid kit to take with you and patch yourself up."

I nod, and once things have settled in the room, I grab the kit from Mr. Smith and leave with my cousin.

"You gonna tell me what that was about?" Santino asks as we make our way across campus. It's finally getting a little warmer out.

"I don't like the way he looks at my fiancée."

Santino nods. "How's that?"

"Like he either wants to fuck her or fight her." We veer to the right on the path that will lead us toward the dormitories.

"Guess he had it coming then."

"Yup." I'm not explaining myself any further.

"Things seem like they're going well with you two. Don't see you guys around much at night . . ."

I know he's fishing, probably wondering where we are. Truth is, a lot of nights we're out at the caretaker's place, either hanging out or banging like fucking rabbits. Seems neither of us can get enough of each other.

"We're busy" is all I say.

He chuckles. "Yeah, I bet."

We walk in silence for a minute, and I ask him what I've been wondering for a while. "What do you think of her?"

He sighs. "I'll admit that I couldn't see how she'd ever fit in when your engagement was first announced. I thought for sure you'd be one miserable bastard. But the past few weeks . . . she's grown on me. It helps that she's not such a bitch anymore—"

I grip his arm, stop us, and swing him around to face me.

"Sorry, man, but you know it's true. You said the same before you were engaged to her."

I remove my hand from him. He's not lying. Only now, I know it was a wall she built up to protect herself. I arch an eyebrow and give him a look that says tread lightly. "And now?"

"And now I think she's okay. With more time, I think she'll fit in fine." He shrugs. "Bianca sure likes her."

I roll my eyes. "Bianca likes everyone."

"True enough."

We walk some more, chatting about Mafia business my father made me privy to on our last phone call, and I spot Polina up ahead of us on the path. She's walking with Irina and Oksana.

I smile as she approaches, and she does the same, but then her face falls. It takes me a second to realize why. The blood on my face.

She rushes ahead of her friends, reaching out as though she

wants to examine the cut and pulling back at the last second. "What happened?"

The rush of affection that fills me at her concern should probably worry me, but I can't find it in me to care. I'm one hundred percent whipped for this woman. I swear hell must have frozen over, and pigs must be flying somewhere.

CHAPTER THIRTY
POLINA

My stomach drops when I see the blood on Dante's face.

Even though I can see he's basically fine, the sight of his blood does something to me, and not because I'm squeamish about blood. It makes me realize how terrified I am for him to be hurt.

He's not exactly in the type of business that's known for its members leading long, full lives, though it's not unheard of. It suddenly hits me that I'm going to be married to a man who always has a target on his back.

I should be used to that. My father and all my brothers have always had the same, but it's different when I consider that this man will be the father of my children, the man I let into my body every night, the only person in this world who really knows me.

"What happened?" I reach toward the cut on his eye and pull back at the last second, not wanting to cause him any further pain.

"Just a little dust-up in combat class." He shrugs as though it's no big deal.

"Are you headed to the medical center? I'll come with you."

"I don't need some nurse fussing over me."

I frown. "You have to make sure you clean it properly so it doesn't get infected."

He steps into me and wraps his arms around my waist. "Is this you offering to be my own personal nurse?" He waggles his eyebrows.

By now, Irina and Oksana have caught up with us. When I look over my shoulder at them, I see them eyeing me warily while Santino keeps an eye on them.

My friends haven't seen too many of our interactions since in public I eat at the Accardi table, not ours. I'm sure it's weird for them to see me like this, especially with Dante. Those walls I fortified for so many years want to come slamming back up with them witnessing this exchange, and I think Dante knows it.

He looks at me expectantly, almost as though he's waiting to see if I step back and put on the mask of indifference that I'm so comfortable with.

But I don't. I just want to be with Dante the way we are when no one is around. Maybe not quite as open, but I'm tired of the old Polina. Keeping up that façade took so much energy, and I don't have it in me anymore.

So rather than brushing him off or saying something cutting, I say, "Not sure. You think I have the bedside manner for it?" I arch an eyebrow.

Dante's smile gleams at me while his hands slip down to my ass. "As long as you promise to kiss all my boo-boos."

"All right, you two, let's keep it decent. We're in public," Santino says good-naturedly.

"Come with me back to my room." Dante's face grows serious.

He knows what a big ask that is. Usually, we spend our time alone at the abandoned house. Going into either of our dorms feels like walking straight into enemy territory without a weapon.

But things have changed for me. While I'm not going to be best friends with any of the Accardis, they haven't been unkind, and I can see us forming a tentative truce down the road. Enough to coexist and maybe even someday be friends.

"Are you sure?" I ask in a low voice.

He nods.

"All right." He squeezes my ass as I turn to face my friends. "I'm going to go back to Dante's with him to help him clean up. Can we hang out tomorrow night instead?"

"Yeah, of course," Oksana says, eyes wide.

Irina just nods. Maybe my brother's shitty attitude is finally rubbing off on her.

"I'm going to leave you guys to it," Santino says to us. "See you around," he says to the girls, who seem surprised that he addressed them.

Dante takes my hand, and we start toward the Roma House. The closer we get, the more I realize what I've agreed to. I have to work hard to keep my breathing even and not let my heart rate get away from me.

"Are you sure this is going to be okay?" I ask as we approach the doors.

He squeezes my hand. "You already know my family isn't going to start shit, and the other families should take their cue from them. Besides, if anyone does start anything, you know I've got you. I'm not going to let anyone hurt you. Why do you think I have this cut on my forehead?" He reaches forward in preparation for swinging open the door.

"What do you mean?" I frown.

"Got this when I kicked Sasha's ass. Didn't like the way he's been looking at you lately and wanted him to know it." He swings open the door and leads me inside.

My stomach bottoms out. Not from the way everyone inside the lounge turns and looks at us, ceasing their conversations, but at the mention of Sasha's name.

What does Dante mean the way he looks at me? Should I even ask, or should I just let it drop?

Dante leads us toward the elevator. Everyone is watching us, and all I hear is the sound of our footfalls. It's like I'm in a horror movie where you keep walking and walking and get no closer to your destination.

When we're about halfway across, a few of the conversations pick up again. By the time Dante presses the elevator button, everyone has turned away from us and gone back to whatever they were doing before we became the sideshow.

When the elevator doors close and we're inside, I release a giant, relieved breath.

"Told you it would be fine," Dante says, squeezing my hand again.

Once we're in his room, he tosses me the first aid kit he has in his other hand. "Here you go. Can't wait for you to display your bedside manner." Then he grins and waggles his eyebrows.

"Never mind about that right now. Go have a seat on the couch. I'll be right back."

"Yes, ma'am," he says jokingly.

I go into the bathroom and wet a washcloth to wipe the blood off his face, then I take it and the first aid kit into the main room. I sit across from him on the coffee table.

"Tell me if it hurts." I gently wipe the blood from his face. The whole time, I feel his gaze on me.

I've decided not to ask about Sasha directly, not wanting to draw myself into a conversation that would force me to outright lie to Dante. There's no way I'm ever going to tell him about my insane plan of seducing Sasha into killing him. But I am curious about what went down.

"Did you at least win?" I ask.

He pulls back from my touch and gives me an "are you serious?" expression. "Is that really even a question?"

I keep quiet. I assumed, but if Sasha getting his ass kicked had anything to do with me, I feel worse than I already did about the whole situation with him.

After I've cleaned the blood off him, I set the washcloth beside me and pull an antiseptic wipe out of the first aid kit. Dante winces when I apply it to the cut, but otherwise he doesn't complain. Then I smooth some Polysporin on the cut and pull out a Band-Aid.

"Are you going to complain if I cover it with a bandage?" I ask.

"What do you think?" He snags the Band-Aid from me and sets it on the table beside the washcloth. "How can I be a big tough Mafia guy with a Band-Aid on my boo-boo?"

I chuckle and bring my hand to his face. "Try not to get into any more fights, okay?"

He kisses the center of my palm the way he always does when I put my hand on his cheek. "You worried about me, tesoro?"

"Yeah, it's a new thing for me. I don't really like this whole having a heart thing." I give him a small smile.

"I know exactly what you mean." Then his hands are on my cheeks, and he's pulling me forward to straddle him.

I end up showing him that I have the best bedside manner of any nurse he's ever had, and I kiss all his boo-boos twice because a good nurse is always thorough.

CHAPTER THIRTY-ONE

DANTE

We're at another party at the abandoned caretaker's house again, and the difference between this one and the last is that this time, Polina arrives with me, hand in hand.

By now, no one really gives us a second look. They're used to seeing us together at this point. We've made no secret of the fact that we are indeed a real couple, not just two people arranged to be married to each other.

"You want something to drink?" I ask Polina once we've found the rest of my crew just outside the kitchen.

"Sure, I'll take vodka with whatever if there's decent vodka. Otherwise just beer."

I shake my head. "Vodka snob."

She trails her finger down my chest. "I seem to recall someone complaining that the pasta we were served at one of the restaurants in California sucked because there was no way it was made fresh like their sign claimed."

I grin and place a chaste kiss on her lips. "Touché. All right, I'll be right back."

In fact, the only things up for grabs tonight are rye or beer from the keg, so I pour us both a beer. When I return, Polina's talking to Bianca. I can't hear what about because the music is pumping too loudly, but she looks relaxed and at ease as I pass her the beer. She gives me a smile but continues her conversation.

We hang out for a while before Dom steps over to us. "Polina, you want to be my partner in a round of beer pong? I'm next up on the table."

I saw the beer pong setup earlier when I went in to refill our beer. Someone somehow got an old dining room table in here and set it up in the kitchen.

Polina looks surprised at first that he's asked her, then pleased. She looks at me as though checking to see if I have a problem with it. I motion to her that it's her decision.

"I've never played before," she says to Dom over the music.

He shrugs. "Whatever. It's easy to learn. I can teach you."

She smiles. "Then sure."

"All right, let's head in there then. They're just about done." He nods toward the kitchen.

I take Polina's hand, and we follow my brother into the kitchen where a set of Irishmen are shaking hands and telling each other good game. Dom steps over to the table and sets up new cups in the shape of a triangle, then takes a full cup of beer and pours some into each of the cups on each side. Rinse and repeat until all the cups are half full.

While he does that, I explain to Polina that the object of the game is to bounce the Ping-Pong ball off the table into the opposing team's cups. If you do, they have to drink the beer in the cup, and whoever gets all the cups on the other side empty first, wins. It gets harder as you go if the other team is always scoring on you because you get progressively drunk.

After Dom has everything set up, he turns back to us. "Dante explain everything? You good to go?"

Polina nods. "Yep, I get it. Not sure whether I'll be any good, but I know the rules." She lets out a nervous laugh, and I wrap my arm around her shoulders and squeeze her into my side.

"Perfect. Now we just have to find someone to play with." Dom whips around and puts his hands around his mouth and shouts, "Who wants to play us at beer pong?"

Like the seas parting, Isabelle steps through the crowd with her hand raised. "I will." She gives a sort of smirk in Polina's direction then looks around for a partner.

I stiffen. I haven't seen too much of Isabelle lately. She got the message when I told her to back off, and I'm sure she's seen and heard all about how well Polina and I are doing.

Santino is talking with some of the Italians. Isabelle wrenches his arm to the side, spilling his beer. "Come be my teammate for beer pong."

He scowls at her, looking down at his hand that's now covered in dripping beer. "The fuck, Isabelle?"

She rolls her eyes. "C'mon."

He looks at us a little warily as she leads him to the opposite side of the table.

I turn my head and say into Polina's ear, "You good?"

She doesn't take her eyes off Isabelle. "Oh yeah. I can handle this."

I chuckle and step back. I'm sure Polina, as a previous mean girl, can handle this, but if Isabelle shows any blatant disrespect to my fiancée, I plan to step in. Maybe Isabelle is just trying to start things off fresh with Polina, but I doubt it.

The game starts off well with Dom and Polina scoring three times to Isabelle and Santino's two.

There's no way to wipe the smile from my face as Polina laughs and carries on with my brother, poking fun at herself when she throws a terrible shot. In some weird way, it feels as though she's always been a part of our family.

Dom grips Polina's shoulders from behind, squeezing and giving her a pep talk about how she's got this. If any other man had their hands on her, I'd cut them off, but I know my brother would never cross any line where my fiancée is concerned.

She nods, and Dom steps back. Polina lines up her shot and tosses the ball. It bounces off the table into one of the plastic cups of beer on the other end of the table.

"Yeah!" Her arms fly up in celebration.

Dom grips Polina's shoulder and shakes it while cheering right along with her.

"That's bullshit," Isabelle says.

We all turn our attention to her.

"She leaned way over before she threw that shot. She was practically on our side."

"You're the one who's full of bullshit, and you know it," Dom says.

"You're going to side with a fucking *Russian* now?" Isabelle spits out, crossing her arms.

The attention of some of the other people in the kitchen turns our way. I move forward, but Polina's hand lands on my chest.

"I've got this," she says, then turns to look at Isabelle. "This isn't the first jealous bitch I've ever had to deal with."

Isabelle's face turns red, and her arms drop to her sides in tight fists. "Why don't you go back to where you belong, Bratva brat?"

Polina's chin tilts up, and she steps around the table, walking closer to Isabelle. Santino is now essentially between them, and he looks at me, seeing if I want him to jump in. I give a slight shake of my head, and his eyes widen. I want to see how this plays out.

"You may not like that I'm engaged to Dante, you probably like it even less that your fuck boy's been taken away from you, but know one thing—I am where I belong, and that's at Dante's side. You may not like it, but I'm his, and he's mine, so back the fuck off. You only get one warning with me, little girl. Stop pouting like a toddler whose favorite toy was taken away and get over it. Do I make myself clear?"

I cover my mouth, because what a fucking queen. I couldn't want her any more than I do right now. My dick is hard, and I don't bother trying to hide it.

Isabelle looks suitably chastised. Santino's clearly trying to keep himself from laughing, and Dom looks at Polina like a proud brother.

When Isabelle doesn't respond, Polina says, "Answer me."

Isabelle's gaze falters, and she looks at the floor. "It's clear."

My badass of a future wife nods like fucking royalty. "Good."

Then she turns and heads back in my direction. The minute she's close enough, I snag her hand and drag her out of the room.

"Game's over," I shout over my shoulder, leading her to the stairs then up to the usual bedroom where we had our rendezvous. The moment we're inside, I slam the door and lock it. "Fuck, it's a turn-on watching you get territorial over me."

She smirks. "You like that?"

I step into her and pull her up by the thighs. She wraps her legs around my waist, and I shift my hands to her ass.

"Grind on the proof, baby." I thrust her against my hard length that's pressing painfully against my pants.

Polina's head falls back, and she moans.

"That was so hot, tesoro."

Then I walk us forward until her back is pressed against the wall. When she rights her head, I press my lips to hers and kiss her deeply, thoroughly, and a little frantically. Because if I don't get inside this woman in the next couple of minutes, I'm pretty sure I might blow my load in my pants.

"You're a fucking queen."

Thank God it's a little warmer out tonight, and Polina is wearing a skirt. I'm not sure I could wait the extra minute it would take me to remove her pants. My mouth trails to her jaw while one hand moves between us, sliding her underwear aside and finding her already soaked and ready.

"Fuck." I nip at her earlobe, and she moans.

Frantically, I undo my pants, lowering the zipper and pushing them and my boxer briefs down until my cock springs free. Then I'm shoving into her in one thrust, and she cries out. Her legs tighten around my waist, and her nails dig into my shoulders.

"You good?" I ask.

"Don't stop." She arches her hips for emphasis.

I plunge into her like an animal possessed and intent on getting his seed into her womb. She takes it, moaning and grappling at me the whole time. Our coupling is frenzied, as though her possessiveness has brought us both down to our base needs.

Polina's back shifts up and down the wall with every one of my thrusts, and she pulls my head down to hers. We don't so much kiss as hold our mouths together as we climb the mountain, searching for the summit.

It's not long until my balls tighten up, and the tingling at the base of my spine tells me I'm going to come soon. Taking a step back, I change the angle as I drive into her, and she instinctively uses her shoulders as leverage against the wall.

I stare at where we're joined as I continue to pump in and out of her. "Just look at you taking my big fat cock into your cunt. I wish you could see what I do, tesoro. It's a beautiful fucking thing. Perfetto."

She cries out at my words. By now I know what gets her off, and I can't help the smirk that curves the corners of my lips as I watch the evidence of her arousal glistening on my dick every time I pull out of her.

"I want you to work yourself on my cock like the little slut you are. Can you do that?"

She nods a little frantically. "Yes, yes!"

I hold still and watch as she moves her hips, working me in and out of her.

"That's a good girl. Just like that, just like that . . . that's my girl." I bring my thumb to her clit and rub in small circles, slowly increasing the pressure until she stiffens.

Her back bows and she finishes, shouting my name. Unable to hold off any longer, I step forward so that she again has the entirety of her back against the wall. I slam into her, head tucked into the crevice of her neck while the slapping sound of our joining fills the room. I spill into her on a roar, holding myself there until she's milked every last drop from me.

Once I've caught my breath, I right my head and kiss her forehead. "I miss this room."

"Maybe we should still sneak off here sometimes even though we make good use of your dorm room now." She looks up at me with sated eyes and a lazy smile.

"Maybe we should."

We kiss as I grow hard inside her again, so we decide to spend the remainder of the night holed up in that room.

CHAPTER THIRTY-TWO
POLINA

"Ugh, I don't want to go," I groan, pulling the covers over my head.

It's Sunday afternoon, and Dmitri has summoned me to his room. I have no idea why. Maybe he learned something on his call today that concerns me, though I have no idea what that would have been. I'm not really involved in the business.

"It probably won't take that long," Dante says, tugging the covers down from over my head.

"I know, but I'd rather stay here with you." I roll my naked body onto his.

He gives a pained sort of groan, then forces me off of him. "I'd rather that, too, but my tongue and my fingers and my dick will be here when you return."

"Promise?" I trail a hand down his chest, then lower, but right before I wrap my fingers around his base, he snatches my wrist and pulls my hand up. I pout, and he laughs.

"Get dressed and go, and when you get back, I'll reward you."

"Hmm, this sounds interesting. What will I get?"

He chuckles. I love that sound. It's my favorite, besides the sound he makes when he comes, which is a deep groan that sort of sounds like a growl. It's like porn for my ears.

"What does my good girl want?" He arches an eyebrow.

My insides clench at his words. I basically melt into a puddle every time he calls me his good girl. It's obscene.

"What I want is for you to do whatever you want to do to me for the rest of the afternoon."

He grins, his light blue eyes flashing, then he takes my nipple into his mouth, biting gently. "It's a deal," he says around my rigid peak. "Just remember you asked for it."

My hands stroke through the waves in his hair. "You need to stop doing that, or there's no way I'm leaving this bed."

He chuckles against my breast and rolls the opposite way, right out of bed. He stands there completely naked, erection in full force and full of confidence. Why wouldn't he be? The man is perfection on every level.

I give him another pout, and he shakes his head at me. "Go see what your brother wants. I'll be here when you get back."

He saunters into the bathroom, and I get a perfect view of his tight ass. I sigh, blowing out a long breath and staring at the ceiling, finding the will to get out of bed.

It's been so nice being in my Dante bubble. Why do I feel like whatever this meeting is about will burst it?

With a muttered curse, I pull back the blankets and get out of bed to get dressed. The sooner I get this over with, the sooner I can come back and be Dante's good girl.

* * *

I KNOCK ON Dmitri's dorm room door. Being back at Moskva House feels weird because I don't spend much time here anymore. In some ways, I feel more at home in Roma House. No one even pays me any extra attention there now when I come and go, and I no longer feel the need for Dante to accompany me through the lobby.

The door swings open, and my brother smiles at me, pulling me in for a hug. "How are you?"

Being in his arms feels good. I realize now how much I miss the close relationship I used to have with Dmitri. We drifted apart when he first became the head of the Bratva and even more when I was pissed at him for pairing me with Dante. Since I've hardly seen him in months, we haven't had a chance to repair our relationship and get back to the way we used to be. I need to try harder with him. He's the one sibling I want to be a part of my life moving forward, and I can't let us fall by the wayside.

"I'm good. It feels like forever since I've really seen you." I smile and walk into the room, coming to an abrupt stop when I find Pavel seated on the couch. The smile drops from my face, replaced with unease. "Hey."

He gives me a chin nod as a hello, and I walk to the far side of the couch he's sitting on and take a seat. Dmitri takes the chair from his desk and sits opposite us on the other side of the coffee table.

"So, what's this about?" I ask Dmitri, not bothering to look at Pavel though I feel him studying me.

Dmitri looks serious. "I wanted to let you know what the most recent report from the outside world had to say."

I blink a few times. That was not what I expected to hear. "Okay . . ."

"Seems this engagement with Dante has done what we'd hoped it would do. Tensions have lessened, and there hasn't been any action from either side in weeks. Even here at school, things have calmed down in recent weeks. I'm sure you've both noticed."

Pavel grunts beside me, but I nod. "I did, actually."

"It's still a tentative peace to be sure, but it's a start. Now we can all get back to doing what we do best—making money—instead of worrying about who might ambush who when."

"That's great." I'm not sure why he felt the need to have a special meeting about it, but I'm relieved that it's nothing more than this.

"It is. And we have you to thank for it, Polina. I wanted you to know how proud we are of you. Right, Pavel?" He turns his attention to my twin.

I look at Pavel.

"Of course, what's not to be proud of?" His words are what Dmitri wants to hear, but the gleam in his eyes doesn't match them.

Dmitri doesn't seem to notice though. "You really stepped up, sestra. You're not a part of the Bratva in the same way Pavel and I are, but we called on you to make a sacrifice for the family, and you came through. Even if you weren't happy about it at first." He gives me a knowing grin, then chuckles softly and shakes his head. "You made it work and did what needed to be done. I'm proud to call you my sister."

My cheeks burn under his praise because I'm not sure I deserve it. I had my own plan with Sasha, though I called it off, and if Dmitri had paired me up with anyone but Dante, the result would not have been the same. Things are only this good because I've fallen in love with the man.

The air whooshes from my lungs. It's not the first time thoughts like this have floated through my head, but it's the first time I've admitted to myself how I really feel about Dante.

I love him.

The question is, does he love me?

"Polina?"

I blink and focus back on Dmitri. I must've blanked out. "Sorry, yeah?"

"We owe you a debt. Thank you for what you did," Dmitri says.

"You're welcome." It's all I can say.

A quick glance at Pavel tells me he is not happy with all the praise Dmitri is bestowing on me. My stomach clenches.

Dmitri stands and pulls me up to embrace me. This feels good. Maybe this is the first step toward getting our relationship back to where it used to be. Perhaps we both just needed time to settle into our new roles.

I squeeze Dmitri, feeling once again like the little sister he used to love and look out for. When we pull apart, he gives me a smile that makes me think maybe he's thinking the same.

Then he ruins it by looking at Pavel and saying, "You can leave now. I'd like to speak with Polina alone."

Pavel looks between us, obviously unimpressed with being dismissed. Though I'm afraid Dmitri's dismissal will anger Pavel further, I'll be happy when he's no longer here, scowling at me.

I've been lucky since that night by the dorm that he hasn't hurt me again. Maybe he is afraid Dante would catch on if he did. I'm sure he knows by now that Dante and I are sleeping together. There's nowhere on my body to hide the bruises anymore, even as strategic as Pavel always is with where he inflicts pain.

"What do you have to tell her that you can't say in front of me?" Pavel snipes.

"I gave you an order." Dmitri's voice is as unbending as steel, something I'm not used to hearing from him.

Pavel stands and shakes his head before leaving, slamming the door as he does and making me startle.

"He'll get over it," Dmitri says, but I'm not sure he will.

It's just one more slight that Pavel will pile onto his list of reasons he resents me.

"What did you want to talk to me about?"

Dmitri frowns, pushing a hand through his hair. "This has to stay between us. The only reason I'm even trusting you with this information is because I think you should know what's at stake. You have to understand how important it is that you make this work with Dante."

My forehead creases. What is he talking about? "Okay . . ."

"The Italians, specifically the Vitales, have something on us—on Feliks more specifically—that cannot come out. It's part of the reason I agreed for you to be wed to Dante Accardi."

A sharp stab of pain centers in my chest at hearing my dead

brother's name. I try not to think about him too much, and when I do, I push those thoughts to the back of my mind. "What do they have that could be so bad you're afraid for it to come out when Feliks is already dead?"

Dmitri places his hands on his hips and gives me a serious look. "It's a video of Feliks and myself planning the assassination of Alexander Kovalchuk."

I stare at him for a beat, too shocked to say anything.

Alexander Kovalchuk was the leader of the Bratva prior to Feliks taking over. He had no heirs, so when he died, it was uncertain for a time who would step up to lead. But when Feliks stepped up and tracked down those responsible for killing Kovalchuk, the members unanimously decided who should take over. At least, that's what Feliks said he'd done . . .

The hierarchy in the Bratva isn't quite the same as it is in the Italian culture. In the latter, the son always takes the place of the father. While that can happen with the Bratva, there's also an element of the strongest shall survive, and if members don't think you're the one who should run it, it can make things . . . difficult.

If anyone found out that my brothers killed Kovalchuk and pretended to be the heroes who avenged him . . . I don't have to ask to know what would happen to them, to me even.

I swallow hard. "I don't want to know any other details."

"Good, it's better that way. But now you understand why I had to agree to the arrangement. I knew you wouldn't be happy about it, but I did feel your marriage could help settle things between the two sides. I'm just glad you've settled into your role, and I needed you to understand the importance of it remaining that way."

I nod absentmindedly as the news settles in. I knew Feliks wanted more power, but I had no idea the lengths he'd go to get it.

"I didn't expect to find myself in this position, running things, but what's done is done." There's a sadness to his words, and I know he's also thinking of our brother. Losing him was likely doubly hard for Dmitri. He was never the one who wanted to run things, and now he's been thrust into that role. "I'm sorry I couldn't put you first when it came to this situation."

I hug him again, tears in my eyes. "I understand now. I do. Your secret is safe with me."

No part of me feels good about having to keep this from Dante, but I can't ever tell anyone. It doesn't matter anyway. What we have is real, and this has no effect on my feelings for him.

"What should I tell Dante when he asks why you wanted to see me?"

"Tell him the first part of the meeting, then tell him I'm pressuring you to set a date for this summer and to start making your wedding plans."

I give him a sad smile. I've started thinking about it myself—where we should have it, what kind of dress I want to wear. I'm actually excited about our wedding, something I couldn't have even fathomed months ago.

"All right. I'd better get back, though. Thank you for trusting me and telling me." *Thank you for being the big brother I know and love again.* But I don't say it.

He winks. "You know you're my favorite sibling."

His words remind me of the look in Pavel's eyes before he left, because he knows it, too.

CHAPTER THIRTY-THREE
DANTE

You'd think you wouldn't miss someone who's on the other side of the room from you, but you'd be wrong.

Polina's sitting at the Aminoff table for dinner tonight. In the days since she went to meet her brother, I've noticed she's spent a little more time with him, stopping by the table to say hello whenever she's eating with me. But tonight, she wanted to sit with her family, something I respect, even if I prefer her with me.

"Are you seriously that pussy-whipped that you can't take your eyes off her for two minutes?" Santino says, drawing my attention back to him.

"I was paying attention." I shove a forkful of salmon in my mouth.

"Bullshit. What was I saying then?" he asks, leaning back and folding his arms over his chest.

"Something boring as fuck, hence me not listening."

He shakes his head and rolls his eyes. "Never thought I'd see the day Dante Accardi was in love."

It's on the tip of my tongue to deny the allegation, but who am I kidding? I'm completely owned by this woman, only I haven't told her yet.

All of a sudden, I have the pressing need to proclaim my love for Polina. I don't want to wait another minute. She should know there's nothing I wouldn't do for her, nothing I don't love about her, even her prickly side.

Pulling my phone from my pocket, I type out a text to her.

> **ME:** Meet me at our spot in forty-five minutes.

I set my phone on the table beside my plate and look over my shoulder, wanting to see her reaction when she reads it. But she's not at the table anymore, though I see her phone on the table. When I look at the large doorway that leads to the space where the food is served, I spy her long blond locks. Must have gone back for dessert.

I smile, knowing I'll be having her for dessert tonight.

Bianca joins us at the table after chatting with Aria Vitale in the food line. Those two are still close. Bianca befriended her as soon as she showed up on campus, and they've remained friends even though Aria is now married to the head of the Vitale family and expecting his child.

I knew she had to be knocked up when they had a rush wedding at Thanksgiving.

"Oh my god, did you guys hear the latest?" Bianca says once she's seated.

"You are such a gossip." Dom tosses a piece of bread at her, which she dodges.

She gives him a snarky look. "Don't pretend you don't love it. You wouldn't know half the shit that goes on around here if it weren't for me."

"What's going on?" I ask before the two of them can get into it. They're more like siblings than cousins. I don't think Dom even bickers this much with Lucia when we're home.

"Apparently Mr. Smith disappeared."

I frown. "What do you mean he disappeared?"

"He disappeared. People showed up for their class with him today, and he wasn't there. Someone from the administration went to check on him, and apparently his entire place was empty. It's like he was never even there."

"Did someone take him out?" Santino asks.

It's not inconceivable. Despite the school's no-violence policy, people have died on campus before. The past couple of years have been brutal. Most times, it's covered up. Someone just goes missing, never to be seen again, and they have no real proof as to what happened.

Like what happened with Polina's older brother and a couple members of his crew last semester.

"Why would someone take him out?" Bianca asks. "He's just a teacher."

Santino, Dom, and I share a look.

She's a girl, so she's never gotten to take Mr. Smith's classes. He only taught weaponry and combat skills. But the guys who have dealt with him over the years know there's something about him . . . something that's always made us feel as though there's more to him than meets the eye.

I think the only reason the girls around campus know who he is, is because they think he's hot. I've heard them going on and on about it more than once.

"Maybe," I say. "But why would his entire place be wiped clean? Feels more like he wanted to disappear for some reason."

My phone buzzes on the table, and I lift it to see that Polina has texted me back.

TESORO: Can't wait. I'm going to get a head start.

I look over my shoulder to find her smiling at me and standing from the table, obviously saying her goodbyes. My dick twitches as

I think of what I'm going to get her to do with that mouth at the house.

"We lost him again," Santino says.

I turn back his way and glare at him. We chat for another few minutes, throwing around theories about what might have happened to Mr. Smith. When I take another glance back at the Aminoff table, I see that Polina is long gone, so I stand, picking up my tray.

"I gotta run. I'll see you guys later."

"Say hi to Polina for us," Santino says with a shit-eating grin.

"Fuck off."

I head for the other section where the food is served to return my tray and dirty dishes. I'm just going through the doorway when Pavel steps into my path, bumping into me with a tray full of food and spilling tomato soup all over me.

"What the fuck, stronzo?" I barely keep my fury in check. I'm well aware of what a piece of shit he is, but to anyone looking, he's my future brother-in-law.

"Apologies. Didn't see you there." The smirk on his face says otherwise.

I suppose this is payback for when I confronted him. Whatever. I'm happy to let him have it as long as he doesn't fuck with Polina anymore.

"Yeah, I'm sure you didn't." A quick glance around tells me we've drawn attention to ourselves. With food dripping down my shirt onto my pants, the heat from the soup stinging my chest, I squeeze his shoulder. Much harder than necessary, but you wouldn't know it from my relaxed smile. "Don't worry about it. Accidents happen."

It's apparent from the grimace on his face that I'm hurting him. Good. How does he like it?

"That they do." Pavel turns and drops his now-empty tray where they go, then walks past me.

Fucker didn't even bother to pick up his dishes scattered across the floor.

I squat and pick up the dishes. Now I'm going to have to walk to the other side of campus and change before I meet Polina. Once I've taken care of the dishes, I fire off a quick text to Polina, letting her know I'll be a little late.

I don't bother telling her why. Mentioning her brother will only upset her.

CHAPTER THIRTY-FOUR
POLINA

It's been a bit since we've met here now that we're usually at Roma House, but I get a little thrill every time we do. It feels nostalgic and like our own little secret.

I think tonight might be the night I tell Dante that I love him. I've been holding off, but I'm pretty sure he feels the same. And this is the perfect place to do it since it's the first place we really made love.

Since Dante has been held up for some reason, I take it upon myself to make the room ripe for romance. I pull out the blankets and the candles we hid in the closet and get them all set up. Once I'm happy with it, I light all the candles.

The windows up here are all boarded up, so they don't let in any light from the outside. A warm glow flickers on all the walls once the candles are lit, creating a pattern of shadows. I know from experience that the candles only emphasize the ripples in Dante's abdomen, and I decide that I might spend a little extra time exploring them with my tongue when he shows up.

The sound of footsteps on the stairs makes me smile, and my heart rate picks up in anticipation of hearing Dante call me his good girl.

"I thought you were going to be late?" I call, smiling and waiting for him to appear in the doorway.

But the silhouette of the person standing there is not my fiancé. It's my worst nightmare.

"Oh, I'm right on time," Pavel says.

I take a couple of steps back. "What are you doing here?" I try to keep my voice strong and not let on how bothered I am by his presence, but I don't think I succeed.

"Can't a brother have a little visit with his sister?" He steps forward.

I take another two back. I'm in the middle of all the candles now, standing on the blanket. "What do you want, Pavel?"

He looks unhinged. His eyes are wide with a strange gleam, and he has a creepy smile, as if he wants to cut me into pieces. "I've been waiting, biding my time, knowing if I did, it would pay off. And when you were stupid enough to leave your phone on the table when you went back to get dessert, I saw the text from Dante asking you to meet him here."

I try to remember what Dante's text said. My thoughts are racing, but I don't think he said specifically where to meet him.

"I can see you're trying to figure out how I knew that he meant here. Let me save your little brain the effort. You two aren't as stealthy as you think. You're always so wrapped up in each other that you never noticed when I followed you here."

My hand goes to my stomach as the sick feeling rises. All the hair on my arms and the back of my neck rises.

"Yeah, I know you two are using this place as your little love shack." He glances around. "You'd think the heir to the Accardi family could do better than this piece-of-shit room."

I raise my chin, trying to adopt that unaffected air that was once so natural to me. "Dante will be here any minute. You should go."

He laughs, and the sound makes me cringe; it's so unnatural. "Dante's been delayed."

My cool expression falters.

"But I'm sure you know that already, don't you? He would have texted you. Did he tell you I'm the one who made him late?"

I don't know what to do. What to say. I have no idea how long Dante will be. He didn't say why he was going to be late. My phone is in my back pocket. I could call Dante for help, but if he's still on the main part of campus, he'll never get here before Pavel does whatever he's here to do. No, I'm better trying to de-escalate this situation.

He still hasn't said why he's here, but something tells me that tonight he plans to go further than just hurting me.

"What do you want then? You still haven't said." I manage to keep my voice even this time.

Pavel steps forward, but I hold my ground. "I want you to pay for how miserable you've made my life."

I blink several times as fury roars through me. Fury I'm unable to hold back. "I made your life miserable? You've been hurting me, torturing me for over a decade. You're my twin brother, and all you've ever done is hate me, say cruel things to me, and physically abuse me. How have I made *your* life miserable?" By the time I've finished my tirade, I'm yelling.

"You little bitch. You don't even see, it's such a part of you. All your manipulations where everyone in our family is concerned." His hands fist, and he takes another step forward. "All you had to do was smile in Dad's direction, and he'd give you whatever you wanted, his little princess who could do no wrong, who got all the attention and the praise. The only daughter. And then there was me, the third son. Barely acknowledged, and when I was, it was only so he could tell me what I'd done wrong."

My head shakes. "You're nuts. Papa loved you as much as he did me."

Another sick-sounding chuckle leaves him. "He didn't give a shit about me. All his time and attention were spent on Feliks and Dmitri. And you talk about us being twins? You were always closer with Dmitri than you were with me!"

"That's because he doesn't find pleasure in hurting me!" I shout.

"Bullshit. It was even before that, and you know it."

I cast my mind back, trying to remember. It's true, in part because Dmitri was older and took me under his wing, looking out for me even when I was young. But that didn't mean I didn't love Pavel, at least back then.

"So, what's the plan? You're just going to kill me, and in turn, have Dmitri kill you? Doesn't seem like such a sound plan to me." It's a small miracle that I manage to keep my voice from breaking.

He reaches into his back pocket and pulls out a pair of gloves, slowly putting them on while not removing his gaze from me. A slow, sadistic grin envelops his face. "No. I'm going to kill you, and Dante will be framed for it. Once you're dead, I'll send myself a text from you begging me to come here to help you because Dante is angry and scaring you."

My heart stutters. "That will never work. Everyone on campus knows we care for each other." But even I hear the doubt in my voice.

He takes another step closer, and I take one back, just missing one of the candles on the floor. "Do you really think it will be that hard for our fellow Russians to believe that Dante turned on you and killed you? That this lovey-dovey shit you've got going on was just an act on his part?"

My heart hammers so hard I have to strain to hear him over the sound of it.

"Pavel, you don't have to do this," I whisper, inching back.

"Oh, yes I do, and I'm going to enjoy every moment." And then he lunges at me.

CHAPTER THIRTY-FIVE
DANTE

The moment I step onto the front porch of the abandoned house, I sense that something is amiss. Years of honing my instincts to alert me to the ever-present danger in my life, I suppose.

So rather than barreling up the stairs as I had planned—I jogged here so I wouldn't keep Polina waiting long—I creep into the house and quietly make my way up the stairs. Every creak makes me cringe, and when I get about halfway up, I hear voices.

Polina's for sure and a man's . . .

When he speaks again, I realize it's Pavel. I can't make out what he's saying, but I'm sure it's him.

Fire erupts in my veins as if my blood is gasoline because whatever the reason he's here, it isn't good. I crest the stairs and walk toward the room, choosing speed over silence now.

I have no idea what the situation is. Does he have a gun? A knife?

The moment I move into the doorway, I see him lunging toward a terrified Polina.

"I thought I told you to stay the fuck away from my fiancée."

Pavel stills and looks over his shoulder. Polina tries to use the opportunity to get past him, but he snags her around the waist and pulls her toward him. She yelps and fights him, but he's too strong and doesn't let go.

I notice the gloves on his hands, and my hands itch to rain down punishment on him.

"I wasn't expecting you until a little later," he says.

"Sorry to ruin your plan." I take several steps into the room.

"Don't come any closer, or I'll break her neck."

He could do it, too. By the time I reached them, it would be too late.

Fear causes a cold sweat to break out on my body, but I push it back. Generally, when I'm in these kinds of situations, I don't have so much to lose. My life, sure, but I made my peace a long time ago that when it's my time, it's my time.

But seeing the woman I love in danger brings about a different sort of panic and fear. If I allow it to overtake me, I won't think clearly.

A quick glance around the room tells me I don't have many options as far as weapons go. When I see the candles flickering around the blankets, I get an idea I think can work. But I need to make sure Polina is safe first.

"Why are you doing this?" I speak to buy myself some time, trying to figure out how to get Polina away from him. I meet her scared gaze and try to communicate with my eyes that we're going to be okay. I'm getting her out of this. When I promised her I'd protect her, I meant it.

Pavel laughs, and it sounds as if he may have lost it. "She sure did a number on you, didn't she? Typical of her. Here you are wanting to save your intended bride when you'd probably want to snap her neck, too, if you knew what she had planned for you."

Polina stiffens, and my stomach sours. From her reaction, whatever he's about to spew at me has at least some truth to it.

"That's right, sis. After Sasha left your room that night, I cornered him, and he was so angry . . . so heartbroken. It barely took any effort to get him to tell me what you'd done. Trying to seduce another man into killing your fiancé . . ." he tsks.

Sasha was in her room? Seducing another man . . .

Polina's eyes fall to me, pleading.

"What the fuck?" I ask.

"It's not how it sounds," she says.

Pavel jostles her abruptly. "Don't try to sweet-talk him. It's exactly what it sounds like. She had Sasha eating out of the palm of her hand, thinking she wanted to be with him. Had him willing to try to take you out to get you out of the way, isn't that right?"

Tears well in Polina's eyes.

"Admit to it." Pavel tightens his grip on her.

Her body crumbling, she looks at the floor. "Yes," she whispers.

Pain feels like a spear stuck in my chest as I look at the woman I love admitting that she wanted me dead. Even as much as I didn't want to marry her in the beginning, I didn't want to kill her.

I don't know what's going on in her head, but now isn't the time to figure it out. Does she still want me dead? I don't know, but I do know that I can use this development to my advantage.

"You little bitch." I use all the pent-up rage I have inside at Pavel for hurting his sister for years, for wanting to kill her now, and allow it to transform my face. "Was that the plan all along? Lure me in with your pussy, get me to let my guard down, so you could kill me?"

I take an aggressive step forward as though I'm barely holding myself back from hurting her. Pavel doesn't say anything or try to stop me, so I take another one, keeping laser-focused on her face as though I can't see anything else in the room, can't think straight through my fury.

"Answer me!"

Polina cringes at my demand but slowly nods and lifts her head to meet my eyes.

It's hard not to soften when she looks at me with so much pain and regret on her face, but I don't allow an ounce of what I'm really feeling to creep into my expression.

I take another two steps forward while I shout, "Your brother is right about you. Every word he just said. You'd do just about anything for your own gain, wouldn't you? Even suck my cock and let me fuck you like the little slut you are."

The flash of hurt and shame on Polina's face almost makes me crack, but I shore up my defenses against the knowledge that I'm hurting the person I care most about. It has to be done.

With another step forward, I put my hands out in front of me as though I'm trying not to strangle her.

"What happened? Did you not suck his cock good enough to talk him into taking me out?" I take another step forward. I'm almost close enough now to reach them.

"No! I told him I didn't want him to hurt you. That I changed my mind." Tears stream down her face.

My heart squeezes painfully that she could believe I'd so easily turn on her. Then again, I've never had the opportunity to tell her how I feel.

"Shut up. Stop your fucking crying." Pavel's attention turns to her as he jostles her in his grip.

This may be my only opportunity, so I take it, lunging for him with my fist and hitting him in the jaw. His hand instinctively moves from around Polina to his face.

"Run!" I yell at her.

She looks at me wide-eyed. I push her out of the way just in time for Pavel to come at me. I brace for the impact and manage not to fall to the floor when he tries to sack me like a linebacker. Polina shouts while I rip Pavel off me, and the two of us exchange punches. His don't land with the same impact as mine do since he's wearing gloves.

Pavel's not exactly a pussy, but I bet he'll tire before I do. And he does. After the sixth blow we exchange, his chest heaves, and his punches hold less strength. I tackle him to the floor, straddling him.

"Polina, run!" I shout. I don't want her to see this because even though I don't think she has any love for her brother, Pavel's death will be brutal and gory.

Weapons make for a quick, easy death, but when you have to kill someone with your bare hands, quick and easy aren't an option.

Chancing a quick glance over my shoulder, I see she has her fingers in her mouth, looking uncertain.

"Go!"

This time she does, racing from the room.

Turning back toward Pavel, I center my weight over him so that his arms are pinned, and I punch him in the face—one, two, three times. When he looks dazed enough, I wrap my hands around his neck and squeeze.

He fights back then, twisting and turning underneath me.

Removing one hand from around his neck, I swipe a nearby candle, sending it careening toward one of the boarded-up windows and the ragged, old curtains that hang there. As I'd hoped, it only takes a few seconds for the curtains to catch on fire. The flames start slow, but in less than a minute, they're licking the ceiling.

I keep trying to strangle Pavel, coughing as smoke fills the room. He's desperate now, like a wild animal underneath me. So much so that he almost dislodges me.

With my hands around his neck, I squeeze and at the same time pull him up before slamming the back of his head against the wood floor. I do it again and again until he's either dead or passed out. I can't be sure which.

But I can't stick around to find out. The smoke is becoming suffocating. If I don't get out of here soon, I'll either pass out or be unable to find the door through the smoke. Leaving him, I crawl toward the door. As soon as I'm outside the room, I stand and shut the door, holding on to the door handle since I can't lock the door from the outside.

Pavel must come to because a minute later, he shouts. Then

there's scratching at the bottom of the door, almost as if he either can't stand or won't. I continue to hold the door, pulling it toward me in case Pavel does stand and tries to yank it open. The door handle grows warm then hot, but I just cringe through the pain as I listen to Pavel's screams from inside.

"Dante! Dante!" Polina's voice sounds from downstairs, then she's beside me. "Oh, thank God. I saw the flames from outside."

"You need to get out of here. Go!"

She shakes her head frantically. "I'm not going anywhere without you."

I turn back toward the door, and it's then I realize that I no longer hear Pavel's screams or his banging on the door. Most people who die in fires don't die from burning to death but from smoke inhalation. Looking between the door and Polina, I question whether it's been long enough to kill him.

Smoke billows out from under the door as the handle becomes too hot for me to hold any longer. I release it and shake out my hands, cringing. The fire must have engulfed the entire room by now.

"Your hands." Polina tries to take them, but I yank them away, turning her toward the stairs.

"Let's go before this entire place goes up in flames."

We race down the stairs and out onto the front porch, then down those stairs and far enough away from the house that we can see the entirety of the second floor.

Fire has spread to all the bedrooms now.

"Is he really dead?" Polina whispers.

I take her into my arms. "He is."

Though I probably shouldn't be surprised when she relaxes into my arms, I am. This is the second brother she's lost in a year.

She pulls away and looks up at me. "I know I should probably feel sad about it, but I don't. I only feel relief." Then her face crumples and she cries.

I pull her into my chest, rubbing her back even though it makes my palms sting. I'm sure they're damaged from the doorknob. We remain like that for a minute before she pulls away and looks up at me, placing her hand on my cheek. I turn my head and kiss her palm like I always do when she does that.

Something like relief passes over her face. "What Pavel said in there . . . about Sasha."

I place a finger over her lips. "Did you sleep with him?"

She shakes her head.

"Did you fool around with him at all?"

She shakes her head again.

"Did you really tell him that you didn't want him to kill me?"

Polina nods. "I told him I thought we could be happy together. I still think we could be if you can forgive me."

I cup her face in my hands. "I love you, Polina. Every part of you. The difficult parts, the perfect parts, even the parts I don't fully know yet. There is so much more to you than anyone knows, than you let people see. I feel blessed that you share that part of yourself with me."

Her bottom lip trembles. "You're the only one who's ever really looked, who wanted to see the real me."

"Tesoro, I want all of you. What matters to me is that you made the choice of your own free will to put an end to your plan. That you see what we could be together, too."

She studies my face, almost as if she can't believe the words coming out of my mouth. "I love you, too, Dante. Every part of you."

We come together in a kiss that blazes hotter than the fire currently burning down the house.

When I finally pull away, I kiss her forehead. "We have to get out of here. They'll have seen the smoke at the main campus by now, and we won't be alone for long."

She nods and takes one last look at the house, frowning. "What will we say about Pavel?"

"We won't say anything because we were never here. I'm sure the story from the administration will be that it was an accident. Pavel must have accidentally started the fire and then couldn't find his way out of the room before he was overcome by smoke."

She nods and then looks at me. "And your face? I'm sure you're going to bruise."

I shrug. "I'll tell Santino to say that we were sparring and got carried away. Don't worry."

"Okay."

"Trust me?" I arch an eyebrow.

"Always." She places a chaste kiss on my lips, and then we rush toward our future.

EPILOGUE
POLINA

So far, living in California has been amazing. School ended a couple of months ago, and my mom came out to stay with me for a few weeks to plan the wedding. She's still mourning the loss of Pavel, and I was pretending to as well, so I invited her for an extended visit, hoping to take her mind off of losing two sons in a short period of time.

She'll be returning in a couple of days because I'm marrying Dante in just over a week. I cannot wait.

After everything went down with Pavel and his death was ruled an accident, I spent months pretending I was mourning the loss of another brother. It grated on me, because if people ever knew what he was really like to me, they wouldn't expect me to be sad he was gone.

So the last couple of months at the Sicuro Academy felt long and drawn out, and I just wanted to finish so that I could be back in California with Dante, in our own little bubble.

We closed on our own house last month. In the end, I decided I wanted to live by the beach. It might not always be right for us, but for now, when it's just the two of us, it works.

Dante has continued to try to teach me to surf, and I think I'm finally getting the hang of it. And if we feel like the excitement of downtown, we're not that far away and can always drive in and stay at his family's condo.

I punch in the code to the gate, and Bianca pulls into the driveway of our new home. She and I went out to grab my bridal lingerie for my wedding night and honeymoon.

"Thanks for coming with me today," I say.

"Of course. There's nothing I'd rather do than pick out lingerie for you to wear for a guy who's like my brother."

We both laugh.

Bianca and I have become close since I moved here and have started to spend time together on our own, without anyone else from the family.

"Well, I appreciate it nonetheless." I undo my seat belt and reach into the back to grab my bags. "Do you want to come in for a bit? We can enjoy a glass of wine on the deck or something."

"I have a feeling Dante would prefer I didn't."

I frown. "What do you mean? He loves you. Did you guys get into it or something?" That would be weird. Dante didn't mention anything before I left.

She shakes her head. "Oh, I know he does. Just trust me." She winks.

I have no idea what she's getting at. Maybe she thinks we're going to get it on as soon as I walk through the door or something.

"Okay, well, I'll see you next week for the rehearsal dinner if I don't see you before." I open the door and get out.

"Absolutely! See you then."

I close the door and watch her reverse down the driveway, the gates closing behind her.

Packages in hand, I walk in and set the bags down while I slip off my shoes. I don't want to give Dante even a hint as to what I bought. I want him surprised and drooling and unable to keep his hands off of me.

I step into the main area of the house and out of the foyer, coming to a stop. The living area is filled with my favorite flowers and battery-operated candles. In the center of the room is a makeshift bed made from blankets similar to the ones we used in the abandoned house when we were sneaking around.

Dante is on bended knee just before the blankets, smiling at me. His light blue eyes sparkle, looking even more striking than normal since his skin is darker from being out in the sun.

"What's all this?" My hand rises to my chest where my heart beats as though I'm running a marathon.

"This is my proposal."

I walk forward until I'm standing in front of him. "But we're already engaged. We're getting married next week."

He nods. "True, but you never got a real proposal from me. Or a ring that I picked specifically for you. You deserve both. Not just an arrangement that other people made for us. You deserve to know that I'm in this of my own free will. Because I want to be."

Tears prick my eyes, but I will them not to fall. I want to see every moment of this clearly so that I can relive it over and over throughout the years and tell our children and our grandchildren about it. "Dante . . ."

"Polina Natalia Aminoff, you are the most complex, beautiful, brave, and resilient woman I know. All qualities I know will serve you well to put up with me through the years."

A soft laugh escapes my lips.

"When we were first arranged to be married, I never could have imagined that we'd end up here. Never could have imagined the tenderness that lay under the hard exterior, the caring woman who hid herself behind a wall of steel in order to protect herself. That you gave me the gift of being able to truly know who you are is the biggest blessing of my life. Thank you for loving me the way you do, and know that I will love you with all of me for as long as I'm alive. I will cherish and protect you and gut anyone who tries to harm you."

I laugh again, knowing he's not kidding. This man would do anything for me.

"You are the end game for me. I can't wait to see what life has in store for us, and no matter what it is, I know that with you by my side, I can face it. Will you do me the honor of becoming my wife next week in front of our family and friends?"

He reaches into his pocket and pulls out a huge cushion-cut yellow diamond ring with tapered baguette white diamonds on each side. The thing has to be at least six carats. It's obnoxious in the best way.

So big that I gasp.

When I don't say anything for a beat, his eyes widen. "Polina. Answer."

I laugh, nodding. "Of course I'll become your wife. There's nothing I want more in the world."

"Phew, I was worried there for a second." He takes my left hand and slides off my original engagement ring, tossing it behind him somewhere.

I hear it hit the floor with a ding.

Then he slides on my new engagement ring.

"It's beautiful," I say. "You did good."

"It's Harry Winston." He shrugs. "I know how much you like your designer stuff. And I figured the yellow center stone was a little different, a little showy. Thought you'd love that, too."

Tears of joy run down my face now, and I kneel in front of him. "Not as much as I love you." I place my left hand on his cheek, and he turns to kiss my palm as always.

"Speaking of . . ." He nods toward the pile of blankets behind him. "Care to reenact the first time we made love?"

I beam. "I'd be disappointed if we didn't."

He tugs me down on top of him on the blankets, and we make

love as the sun sets over the ocean beyond the house, bathing us in fiery light.

At one point, I glance out the wall of windows and see the sun glistening off the water. It's beautiful and bright—almost as bright as our future.

Can't get enough of Dante and Polina?
Turn the page for an exclusive bonus scene
from *Craving My Rival* . . .

POLINA

Ten Years Later

It's only been five days, but it feels like I've been waiting a lifetime for my husband to return.

Dante had to attend a meeting with all the heads of the Italian families because of issues that popped up that affected everyone.

Over the past ten years, it's been rare that we're apart for any significant amount of time, but every time I hate it more than the last.

I check my makeup and outfit one last time before heading downstairs to let Mrs. Marino know she can go home.

She's in her fifties and helps me out with the kids during the day so that I can steal away to put some content together. I ended up doing exactly what I told Dante I wanted to, and I have a thriving styling/fashion blog and social media presence. No one knows it's me behind the brand, and I think some of the mystery of that actually added to its success.

Leaving the bedroom I share with Dante, I wind my way through the expansive house to find the kids. After a few years on the beach, we ended up settling in Calabasas to be close to the family and give the kids the space to run around outside without me being paranoid they were going to drown in the ocean.

I find everyone in the backyard. My oldest, Cassio, is on the large jungle gym we installed a couple of years ago. As usual, he's on the swing, pumping his legs to see how high he can go. He's only seven, but I swear I already know that he's going to give me a heart attack. The boy has no fear and, much like his father, says what's on his mind—right or wrong.

Anastasia, our five-year-old daughter, is with Mrs. Marino, in the life-size dollhouse Dante insisted she have when she turned four. It's white and pink and completely feminine, just like our daughter. What can I say? I passed down her appreciation for nice things.

"Mama!" Anastasia spots me and pokes her head out of the window of the dollhouse. "Is Papa home?"

"Not yet, sweetheart. Soon."

The kids have missed their father almost as much as I have.

My stomach flips over on itself. I can't wait for Dante to get home, but at the same time, I'm nervous about the news I have to tell him. I'm not sure how he'll react.

"Do you want to play tea party with us?" Anastasia asks.

"In a minute, lyubov' moya. I'm going to push your brother first to see if we can get him any higher."

"Okay." She shrugs and goes farther back into the dollhouse, where I assume Mrs. Marino is seated uncomfortably at the little table like I've been many times before.

"Yay!" Cassio cheers, stopping his legs from pumping now that he knows I'm coming to help.

I push him a few times and smile when he begins working his legs super hard. His ultimate goal is to go all the way around, but I haven't bothered to explain to him the effects of gravity yet.

"Papa!" Cassio shouts and then jumps off the swing at the highest point.

My heart comes to a standstill in my chest and my hands fly up to my face until I see he's landed safely on the grass and is running toward Dante.

Then Anastasia bounds out of the dollhouse toward her father, her childish giggle ringing through the warm air.

With them coming from different directions, Dante halts where he is and gets down on his haunches, arms opened wide for them.

I wasn't sure what to expect when we had our first child. Dante had shown me a very different side of himself, one he didn't often let the outside world see. Would he do the same with our children, or would he be the stereotypical Mafia father who's emotionally unavailable and believes that hard knocks are the best teacher of all?

But he's only ever been a loving and adoring father to both of our children. In his eyes, they can do no wrong and are the best little boy and little girl ever to be born.

When they reach him within seconds of each other, he lets himself fall onto his back on the grass, one arm slung around each child. Then he tickles them while they attempt to wiggle themselves away, their joined laughter filling me with peace.

The type of peace I didn't really know was possible in this life I was born into.

"Papa, will you play tea party with me?" Anastasia asks him.

"I want you to push me on the swing!" Cassio shouts.

Dante laughs. "Let me say a proper hello to your mother and then I'll do both those things, all right?"

"Okay, Papa!" Anastasia jumps and runs back to the dollhouse, while Cassio heads back to the swing set.

Dante stands, wiping himself off from being on the grass. He's so hot that he makes me ache inside. The years have only honed his features, and I smirk at him as he makes his way over to me.

"I missed you so much, tesoro." He wraps me up in his arms and brings his lips to mine.

"Ew!" Cassio complains when he sees us.

Dante and I both start to laugh against the other's lips.

"Were you a good girl while I was gone?" He slides his hands down to my ass and squeezes.

"Aren't I always a good girl?" I can't help but arch my eyebrow.

He chuckles. "Except when you're a bad, bad girl." He squeezes my ass again.

"Papa!" Anastasia shouts from her dollhouse.

Dante drops his forehead to mine. "We'll pick this up later?"

"Absolutely." I place a chaste kiss on his lips, and when he backs away, he gives me a look that promises he's going to hold me to that.

* * *

LATER THAT EVENING after the kids are in bed, Dante comes into our bedroom, closing the door behind him and meeting me in the en suite where I'm going through my nightly routine.

"That took longer than expected." He comes up behind me, circling my waist with his arms and looking at me over my head through the mirror.

"Kids didn't want to fall asleep?" I rub the last of my moisturizer into my skin.

"Nope. Guess they really missed their dad."

I screw the lid back on my moisturizer and then spin around in his arms. "They aren't the only ones. Let's not make a habit of you being away that long, okay?"

He dips his head and kisses me long and slow. "I don't plan on it."

"How did your meeting *really* go?"

He uses one shoulder to shrug. "Fine. Nothing we can't talk about later. I want to make love to my wife right now."

His words are music to my ears, but . . . "I want that, too, but first we have something to discuss."

He arches back a little to get a better look at me. "Everything okay?"

It's almost sweet the way he's instantly on alert, as though he's ready to eliminate any threat to me or our children in a heartbeat.

I rub my hand over his chest. "Everything is fine. I found something out while you were away, and I wanted to let you know."

A line forms on the bridge of his nose.

Without another word, I slip out of his hold and walk over to the drawer on the far end of the cabinetry, sliding it open and pulling out what's been in there for the past two days that's going to change our lives—for the better.

I set the pregnancy test on the counter in front of my husband.

"Is that . . ." His eyes widen and he turns to look at me.

I nod. "It is."

His hands grip my face, and the pure joy in his eyes makes any lingering nerves I had about telling him about this unexpected event in our lives slide away.

"Tesoro, this is a blessing. How are you feeling?"

"I'm okay. No morning sickness or anything yet."

"How far along are you?" One of his hands drops from my face down to my stomach.

"Coming up on eight weeks. We've been so busy lately that I didn't even realize I'd missed my period. It didn't dawn on me that I could be pregnant until I woke up the first morning you were away, and I felt . . . off. I knew then. Got in with our doctor that afternoon."

Dante chuckles. "Anastasia is going to be pissed she's not the youngest anymore."

We both laugh together because it's true. She basks in the glory of being the youngest and all the attention it gets her from us and the rest of the family.

"I'm glad you're excited. I wasn't sure. It's not like we'd planned to have any more children."

He frowns for a beat. "Of course I'm excited. It's still a blessing, even if it's an unplanned one."

Dante leans in to kiss me, but I place a finger over his lips before they hit their target.

"I'm glad to hear you say that because there's more."

He tilts his head to the side. "What do you mean . . . more?"

"When they did my pregnancy test, my hCG levels were high, so the doctor had me go do an ultrasound . . . we're having twins."

It's an effort not to burst out laughing at the sheer shock and befuddlement on Dante's face right now. It's clear that it takes a moment for the news to settle in.

"Twins?" His voice cracks on the word.

Now I do laugh. "Yup. Can you believe it?"

He joins me in my laughter. "The kids are going to be running this place in no time." Happy tears spring to his eyes as he pulls me into an embrace.

"No doubt." I wrap my arms around the man who is my peace, my joy, my everything.

"We got this," he says, always confident in his ability to handle anything.

But I know he's right. We have each other, we have love, and that will always be enough.

ACKNOWLEDGMENTS

We hope you enjoyed your time at the Sicuro Academy.

It feels as though our time in this world went by in a flash. One minute we were writing Marcelo and Mirabella's story, and the next we were finishing the series with Dante and Polina's story.

We were looking forward to writing Dante's story because he's definitely the most chill of his counterparts, and it was interesting to see how that might play into his story. Especially when he's told he's to wed a Russian. And a woman he labeled as an ice queen at that. Watching him chip away at Polina's icy exterior to reach the person underneath her mask made for the best moment when he realized there was more to her. She'd been hurt by the person she thought she should trust the most, and Dante stood by her side the entire time.

Sometimes we're cast into roles, either by our own doing or how people perceive us, and sometimes those roles aren't who we are. Or maybe they were, but we've changed or grown. Showing people that's not who you are and showing them a part of yourself that they don't expect can be difficult. It takes courage. Dante gave Polina that courage once she felt that she could trust him.

A big thank you to everyone who helped get this book into your hands . . .

Nina and the entire Valentine PR team.

Cassie from Joy Editing for the original line edits.

My Brother's Editor for the original proofreading.

All the bloggers who have read, reviewed, shared, and/or promoted us and our darker side!

Every reader who got this far! We hope you were entertained and looking forward to what's next!

To May Chen and the entire Avon team—you helped us realize a dream, and for that we will be forever thankful. Thank you for your support of this series!

We owe the biggest thanks to Kimberly Brower, our agent, for making the dream of seeing a series of our books on bookstore shelves a reality.

Next on the P. Rayne horizon? Our new world, Midnight Manor! Think fairytale retellings, four brothers, mysteries and darkness, along with plenty of spice! We even threw in some gothic vibes. We promise you, this is a world you don't want to miss!

Ciao,
Piper & Rayne

ABOUT THE AUTHOR

P. RAYNE is the pen name for *USA Today* bestselling author duo Piper Rayne. Under P. Rayne, they write dark, dangerous, and forbidden romance.

DELVE INTO P. RAYNE'S
MAFIA ACADEMY
SERIES

A dark romance series set at a boarding school for the sons and daughters of the most powerful Mafia lords, now with new bonus content exclusive to the print editions.

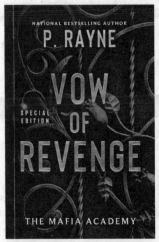

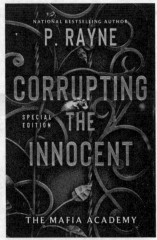

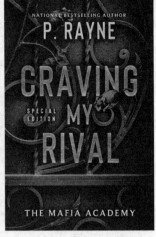